I0766959

New Beginnings

Science Fiction & Fantasy Anthology

Dedicated to our friends,

families, and loved ones

Thank you for all of your help

This section has fancy spacing

Table of Contents

Foreword

Sometimes I wonder if the need for stories is one of the most primal urges people have outside of the basic requirements for survival. It is, after all, one of the oldest activities we can trace. From as long ago as 3,000 B.C., when our ancestors began to sketch organized pictographs onto walls; to the many centuries of oral storytelling throughout the world, be it poetry, song, or verse; to the invention of written language and the printing press; to the transformation of mediums, where stories began to take the shape of graphic novels, radio dramas, television programs, movies, and video games.

It is clear that from time immemorial, people have been creating and recreating stories, but why? To what purpose? Such entertainment does not help us collect water, gather or hunt food, build shelter, keep us safe from threats, or aid in producing more human beings. Yet, it's one of our oldest traditions, something held sacred no matter what form it has taken. Childhood fairy tales. Bedtime stories. Historic myths and legends passed down through various cultures. Ghost stories shared around the campfire. Personal recollections by adults of past exploits and old adventures of youth.

Why do we engage in this activity that does nothing for our physical survival? What do we gain from creativity? Why consume it? Why create it? Why are we drawn to it as naturally as we are drawn to breathe or to eat or to sleep?

Because there is *power* in stories.

Within tales, whether old and classic or new and refashioned, something more within us is fed. Call it whatever you will: our brain, our soul, our heart, our spirituality, that which differentiates us and makes us somehow "other" in this world. Stories speak to that which is within us. We feel the plights of the heroes, connect to them, and sometimes see part of ourselves in them. We cheer for them and, perhaps, use their story to help fuel our own lives, to inspire our actions, to be more like them. In the end, stories influence us, whether consciously or subconsciously. They impart gathered wisdom, teach lessons, give warning, invoke morals, inspire greatness, and ask questions.

The short story, in particular, is one of the oldest forms alongside poetry and song. *Grimm's Fairy Tales. Aesop's Fables. The Canterbury Tales.* Many of the works by authors such as Edgar Allen Poe, Washington Irving, and H. P. Lovecraft. In fact, several of today's most renowned novelists began their careers by cutting their writing teeth on short stories submitted to bygone fantasy and science fiction magazines and anthologies, most notably Stephen King and Isaac Asimov.

It is with all this history in mind – the love of stories, the passion for telling them, the inner calling to create them, and the path laid forward by our predecessors – that we sought to try and resurrect the tradition of the fantasy/science fiction short story anthology. Some may view such an endeavor as baby steps, but, truthfully, there is quite a challenge in attempting to convey a full-length novel's worth of entertainment, meaning, plot, and character development within the confines of a mere few pages. It is also my personal belief that, given the nature of people leading busy lives with less time for indulgences as well as the Internet shaping media consumption into smaller doses, the short story is due for a revival.

We hope that you enjoy our works within and, perhaps, some day you may see longer and more plentiful works by the authors who have contributed to *New Beginnings*.

And now, gentle reader, I leave you with one final thought and blessing: may you always aspire, may you always question, and may the wind always be to thy wings.

-- T. M. Lowe

Living Vicariously

An Eight Fold System Story

Written by

Nicholas Walls

Johnny C. Vid, the man, the marvel, the wonder, looked down the sloping peak with a confident sneer. Stretched out below, his millions of cheering fans seemed like little ants, but even from up here he could hear their roaring adulation. Praising him. Worshipping him.

As well they should. Beneath him lay Death Peak, an artificial mountain and death trap. Beyond lay a full mile of assorted spikes, spinning blades, and firepits, which he, Johnny C. Vid, would jump! Who else would dare such a monumental stunt? Who else but the man himself, El Vid!

Heart pounding in his ears, he ran one last check on his veloci-sled. Inertial dampers check. Engine humming loud enough to rattle his teeth. Grav fields are go. Tension coiled in his stomach, a viper read to pounce.

He was ready.

The instant Johnny released the throttle, a wall of force hit him like the hand of an angry god. Eyes blurring with tears, it took all of his effort to hold the rocket on course, plummeting down the mountain towards the ramp. Then, he was free. Soaring through the air like a chrome-plated angel.

Johnny reveled in the sensation, free and flying. When he reached to ignite the secondary burners, to send him to the other end, he hit a snag. There was nothing there. His hand hit air. Frantic, the daredevil looked down to see a patch of grey nothing, a fuzzy static. Worse... it seemed to be spreading, a burning hole in reality.

Just as the crackling miasma rushed over his eyes, Johnny woke up. He winced as a buzzing noise tried to drill into his brain from both ears. Someone kept shouting at him again and again and again.

"Time up! Time up! Time up!" Unsteadily pushing off the polished chrome table he'd been slouching against, Johnny barely registered disgust at the puddle of drool he'd left behind. With a soft hiss, the cable threading him to the wall plug ejected, whizzing back into the socket beneath his ear fast enough to jerk his head back. Rubbing at the tender flesh around the cybernetic dataport, Johnny glared balefully at the outlet.

The soft embrace of VR, Vicarious Reality, faded, leaving him cold, aware, and subject to the real world's tender mercies. He shuddered as it all settled back on him. He wasn't a daredevil stuntman and this wasn't on any stunt course in a faraway land. He was Johnny C. Vid, strung-out junkie living in The Heap. Currently frequenting Happy Daze, a delightful little dive bar & VR joint that offered about every distraction you could want, for a bit of credit.

Scratching anxiously at the jackport about his neck, Johnny turned to the glowing screen at the back of Daze. On it, larger than life, Obadiah Bidwell reported yet another grisly murder. The shock-jock's obscene relish in recounting the details, ivory tooth grin against obsidian dark skin, robbed it of any sympathy.

Not that it mattered.

None of the other junkies or imbibers in Happy Daze so much as looked up as gore splattered pictures trawled across the wall-sized screen. This was The Heap. No one cared. Just one more life snuffed out.

Johnny might have cared once. Hell, he might even have covered it, a paler copy of Bidwell, chasing wars and murders for a blurb on the news. But that was a lifetime ago. Now, he had more in common with burn-outs, addicts, and junkies in the little dive bar than he did with the shock-jock and his ten-thousand-credit suit.

Wiping dried drool from his mouth and hugging his stained trench coat, Johnny C. Vid shrugged off thoughts of the past and wandered out into the streets to find his next hit.

Johnny walked amidst lights and shadow, through the garbage and castoffs, human and otherwise. Hard-eyed gangers watched him pass, guarding their little corner of urban hell. Burnouts raged at invisible demons. Broken concrete and hyper-steel struts propped up crumbling buildings, but nothing supported the broken hopes, dreams, and bodies of the people living here.

His eyes jerked skyward as another freighter roared overhead through sulfurous clouds. The mighty vessel barely slowed, dumping its castoffs into the growing mounds of junk that gave the place its name before rising again through the halo of smog that encircled the urban sprawl. Miles and mountains of junk, scrap, and unwanted remains. One great shitpile monument to an empire's greatness.

Johnny shook his head and had to fight down the nausea that came with it. The reluctant reality attendant couldn't remember the last time he ate and his whole body ached.

Still, he thought, *a hit of VR will take care of that little problem.*

Knuckles clenched white on his soiled coat, Johnny hurried home.

*****

"Home" in this instance meant a dilapidated flophouse shared by a shifting crew of vagrants. The cast-offs stuck together, bound by necessity and mutual mistrust.

Johnny didn't know the names of half of them. And they didn't know his. And that suited all parties just fine.

What he did know was the little wizened figure talking animatedly to one of his "roommates", ruined teeth in a broad, unfriendly grin. Smiler, Johnny's latest purveyor of Vicarious Reality. Only a pusher would wear a suit that shade of purple. It marked him out like a beacon amongst the bare concrete and drywall.

"Johnny!" the goblin called out, turning to smile at him, all black and yellow and chrome. "What can I do for you?"

"Hey, Smiler. Wondering if you got any of the goods?" Johnny would've cringed at the desperation in his voice, if his need wasn't scratching at him so bad.

It didn't seem possible, but somehow the stunted creature's grin widened further. "I have just the things." He reached into his obnoxious purple suit and pulled a little black box, dotted with colored jacks.

Johnny's mouth watered just looking at it.

Smiler arched an eyebrow. "You know I always got you, Johnny. Good stuff. Primo. Only cost you twice my usual rate."

Damn. No wonder the little shit was smiling. I should bargain and haggle this bastard down. But... I need it. He paused. *Just this once.*

"Sure, sure, I know you're good. And you know I'm good. I just wanna sample the goods before I try them."

The pusher grinned like the Cheshire Cat, amused by a mouse's struggling. "Normally I wouldn't..." A politician couldn't lie so well. "But for one of my best customers..." Gangly fingers plucked out a colored line and held it out with all the reverence and ritual of communion.

Johnny snatched it from him like a starving man at a steak.

Wire slotted behind the ear. Neural feed right through the cords. Through the bone to the spine, round to the brain. Straight hit on the joy buzzer. Direct line to nirvana. But rather than being carried away to a lovely new world, Johnny crashed into a scathing wall of feedback. Static nails on his brain. Muffled echoes of another life wrapped in shattered emotional glass.

Johnny snapped the cable free with a curse. "What the hell are you trying to peddle here, Smiler?" He glared at the little creature who didn't even have the grace to look sheepish.

"What can I say, Johnny? Must have been wired wrong when they recorded it."

The dissatisfied junkie rubbed anxiously at his port, trying to scratch phantom pains. The little shit's story checked out, at first whiff. Damn thing could amateur work; recorded wrong by the person doing the living.

For Vicarious Reality to work, a person had to live it. Another life, on sample and free to taste. Johnny had been a cop, special ops, a lawyer, and even a skin-flick star. But it didn't always take.

Get it wrong, input to output, crossed wires and all you got was brain static. Do it wrong hard enough, often enough, you could slag some pretty vital bits.

But damn if he hadn't gotten a taste of something potent under all that. Only an impression, but real strong. One of the Primals; fear, anger, lust. The junkie wanted it. He wanted it more than he'd even wanted anything in his life. And he knew if he let that slip, Smiler would own him.

Time to see if that time as Johnny the Stud-Poker player is gonna come in handy.

"Even if it wasn't broken, it wasn't half as good as you played it." Sneering, Johnny leaned in on the pusher, despite his protesting nose. "Where did you dig up that amateur hour crap up?"

The Smiler never lost his namesake grin. "Entrepreneurial, eh Johnny boy? I can respect that." He took his client's arm and looked around, suspicious of eavesdroppers. As if any of the deadheads could muster the attention for it. Rule One in The Heap: you mind your own business and look after yourself. "Truth is, all my suppliers been nervous lately, drying up on me. So I found it out in the Boneyard. Primo scrap, primo finds." Again, that grin with more missing teeth than not.

Boneyard. Shit. Johnny felt his stomach drop. Nobody was ever stupid enough to call The Heap safe, but the Boneyard's rep spooked even the locals. A sane man might have reconsidered. But when a junkie needs a hit...

"Yeah? Well thanks for the tip, squib." Johnny shouldered past the riotous clad pusher, driven by need and the last dregs of his pride.

*****

Despite its name, The Heap passed for a city, a place where people worked and lived. If you could call it living. The same couldn't be said of the Boneyard. Birthed of the same mountainous dregs that gave The Heap its name, it marked the beginning of an era... or perhaps the end of one.

Before they expanded into the universe, the human raced used up Old Earth. Rather than learning their lesson, they repeated the pattern, burning through world after world. It took almost a century amongst the stars before the Recyclers and Chem-Rad sanitation nearly removed the need for waste, human or otherwise.

By the time the Illustrious Empire came to rule the Eight Fold System humanity had produced a lot of shit.

Some of it could be recycled, slagged, or molecularly condensed, but not all. There was just too much of it. They couldn't bury it deep enough, couldn't burn it fast enough because the ash and fumes were even worse. So they decided to dump it. Somewhere cheap. Somewhere dingy.

Of course, people protested. They protested and they fought back. But no one important, no one with money, no one with power gave a damn. So a whole city got buried.

The Boneyard. A graveyard to the belief that little people mattered. Too many reminders there used to be people under the scrap. Too many ghosts. Even as the junkpile spread out, eating other cities and becoming the Heap, most folks stayed away. Everyone except the desperate and the crazy.

So that left Johnny, digging through the cast off an empire reaching for the stars. Half the shit was old, non-biodegradable metals and plastics. Not Plas-steel, or ceramite, or hypertension wires. Just... Plastics. Just... metal. Old, useless, worn out, forgotten, and obsolete.

But one man's trash...

Johnny hissed in pain and shook out his hands after scraping them on some rusted-out sheet of metal.

Great. Getting the shakes. Johnny stared at his hands in morbid fascination. *Thought that happened to other people. To junkies.*

He tried to imagine how it came to this. From respected vid-man and finest camera jockey in the business to grubbing through trash for a fix.

Face it, Johnny, you've hit rock bottom. Maybe I'm better off dead.

While Johnny imitated a neo-postmodern Hamlet, an ominous thump and scrape of metal on metal resounded from around the corner of piled debris. A half-life of instincts honed in the slums of The Heap kicked in. Without thinking, he scrambled his bony ass to cover before peeking out from his shabby haven.

Huh. Just like that spy VR bit. Wish I had that tux. Before Johnny's mind became too lost in hazy snippets of stolen memories, something shambled into view.

Something the size of a small mountain. Vaguely man-shaped, but too big and too... uneven. It moved with a limp, thumping ungracefully along. Muscles swollen with stimm glands and bulky as an Auggie, the artificially augmented heavy laborers or warriors found throughout the Empire, but half put together and then abandoned. The thing had none of the sleek lethality of the gene-engineered Corps Hunters or Empress' trained lunatics. Just a lump of unfinished muscle, gristle, and fat.

A thick black apron stretched over worker's coveralls, both straining to keep its bulk in check. Tools and cruel instruments hung about: wrench in a pocket, red tinted surgeon's blade in another. Everything accrued in hell's kingdom.

The thing lazily scanned the area, face hidden behind a stained pig mask. Its rictus caricature of a grinning hog reminded Johnny of Smiler. Rough sutures ran across it, barbed wire stitching holding the rotten material together. A large wet sack hung about its shoulders, flies flicking in and out of it.

It looked like a nightmare birthed from the Boneyard itself.

About this time, Johnny decided he wanted to live.

Just as the hulking brute reached his hiding spot, Johnny darted out past the thing. Pig Face dropped his sack with a wet squelch and reached out with a hand the size of Johnny's head, missing the fleeing junkie by inches.

A terrifying game of cat and mouse ensued amidst the piles and heaps. A deadly game of Tag, with the Pig-Face creature definitely "It." The malformed beast-man chased Johnny through twisting caverns and gullies of trash.

Wish someone could record this chase scene! Just like Driver Johnny did! Move Johnny, move!

Even amidst the terror and thumping heartbeat, Johnny felt a rush as good any of his VR.

That came to a crashing halt when he slammed into a dead end. Hemmed in on three sides by skeletons of cars and aeroships, Johnny looked frantically about. A wet chuckle announced the bone picker catching up to his prey.

Only way... is up!

Without looking back, Johnny scrambled up the piles of metal. Just as he climbed half way up the rusting mountain, a sharp pain tore through his back and tore him savagely from his perch.

A bad joke flashed through the former shock-jock's skull, a remnant from his first and only sky diving adventure: it's not the fall that gets ya... it's the sudden stop at the end.

As a huge shape blocked out the sky, Johnny groggily looked up and saw a length of chain in the monster's hand, ending in a wicked hook.

Sonuvabitch fishhooked me. The last thing Johnny saw was a big, filth-encrusted boot coming down to kiss him goodnight.

*****

Johnny C. Vid woke to an unmerciful scene change, harsher than any of his VR come downs. A vision of hell greeted him.

A metal cavern, lit by flickering florescent strips and foul-smelling lumps of candles. Rust and oil coated everything, red and black stains on stripped metal. Hooks and chains dangled from the ceiling, with people, corpses, and those in between hung from them. A hodgepodge of diner tables, hydraulic lifts, and surgeon's chairs sat in a circle, each one adorned with a bound person. An offering on an altar. Some of the trapped victims moved. Some. A steady drip and buzzing of flies filled the air. Johnny gagged on the charnel house stench. Walls covered in mattresses and construction stripping, brutish sound muffling.

So no one can hear the screams. Johnny tried to leap off the table only to be violently halted by thick leather straps. After slamming back to the table, he managed to move his head about, desperately searching for a way out from this house of horrors.

Their host entered with a creak of rusted hinges and a clang. Without even looking at his victims, he stomped over to a work desk, back turned to the captive audience. Craning his head, Johnny could just see catch his kidnapper out the corner of his eye.

The mask had nothing on the monster's ugly mug. Molted and warped, like clay, muscles twitched and veins bulged. Scars crisscrossed mottled flesh, mirroring the barbed wire of its false face. Tumorous growths completely covered one eye while the other glared about, a dark pit of malice. In all, a killer's face, a beast's face. Brutal and ugly as the pit it dwelt in. And it was looking right at Johnny.

Johnny tried not to panic as the bloody thing shuffled toward him. *Ok ok. Action scene, Boom Boom flick! This is where our hero Johnny gets the drop on him! Just like Commando Johnny!*

A balled fist upside the head interrupted ol' Johnny's inner monologue. Pig-Face slung the dazed man across his shoulder in a fireman's carry. A musk of oil, blood, and chemical sweat hung oppressively about the beast. Johnny fought down a wave of nausea and told himself he was just biding his time, ready to strike... but when the rusty hook tore through his shoulder, a startling and terrifying realization rushed over him... this wasn't an action flick, it's a horror movie and he's the victim.

"Nononono, please, please, please, you can't do this. Don't do this. I'll do anything... don't make me an extra in my own life!" Numb fingers clawed at the chain as the former shock-jock gibbered.

His pleading earned him a push from Pig-Face, sending him swinging. Johnny choked, a panicked gurgle, gulping for air through the pain of the sharp hook digging deeper.

A thrashing from one of the tables diverted his tormentor's attention from his current game. Pig-Face turned from Johnny, a merciful moment of respite. One of the victims thrashed as Pig-Face's cruel devices did their work. Death spasms. The last moments before the lights go out.

Seen too many of those not to recognize it. Bitter memories, too real, washed over Johnny. Fire, blood, and broken bodies; A career spent chasing atrocities beyond count. All the pain and death he hid from in his many VR trips. Pig-Face, looming over the thrashing corpse-to-be, uttered a low chortle, a nasty, satisfied sound. Hanging like a piece of meat, Johnny shivered. *Looks like I am not the only one who knows the Reaper's Shadow.* The beast's hunger was real; slavering like a junkyard dog with a steak. Johnny squinted suspiciously. There was something familiar about that as well.

The bone picker dug about his own skullcase, fishing through the flabs of fat and meat to pull out a brutal-looking spike. With a snort, he plunged it into the victim's jack. Wire to wire, jack to jack, Pig Face's eyes rolled back with a heavy huff of ecstasy, porcine nostrils flaring.

Hung on his chain, Johnny's eyes widened. *I know THAT look too.* A junkie getting his hit. The bastard is getting off by living through their pain.

As the final moments passed and Pig-Face callously dumped the body down a metal chute with no more thought than throwing out the trash, it hit Johnny where the Smiler got his bits. Dead Play. Ghoul Records. Scavenging this bastard's leftovers.

Trapped in a madman's playground, Johnny grabs onto that realization. He uses it to feed his anger, burning away his despair. *I can't die here. I have to kill this bastard. I have to live long enough to punch Smiler in his stupid gob.* Bitterness and hate helped him fight through the agony as he hauled himself around on the hook. Scratching around his brain case, he hastily scrambles to find his jack. Thankfully the skin is thin, the jack puffy, raw, easy to reach. A sign of how far he'd gone down the rabbithole.

Damn, never thought I'd be grateful to be a junkie. He flicked a few physical bits around before mentally running through his cyberware's settings; tiny checkboxes switching off/on behind his eyes. Digital switches going to and fro. Set system to record. Something he swore off since...

Since I started running from life.

His plan kicked in motion, now he just had to set the trap. So Johnny thrashed and choked, wiggling like a fish on a hook. The monster shuffled back, a shark drawn to blood. Johnny could practically hear its thoughts. 'Another? So soon? Why, I really shouldn't... but why turn down a gift?'

C'mon you gluttonous bastard. Just us junkies. Come get your fix. Ungentle hands steadied the dangling captive and Pig-Face plunged a thick spike into Johnny's port, ready to taste the darkness and despair, the sweet suffering. Instead, the creature found itself sucking down static. Caught in a feedback loop, back and forth, like a hall of mirrors in his brain.

Pig-Face howled, squealing like his mask's namesake, and threw Johnny to the side. As the monstrous creature thrashed blindly about his abattoir lair, Johnny struggled to breathe, staring longingly at the shaft. Pain near blinded him.

Sweet merciful stars, never been on the other end of it. Can't stop. Can't pass out. Gotta move. A small eternity passed as he inched along the floor with one good arm. Leaving a trail of crimson behind him, Johnny reached a dirty patch of rubber beneath the chute. Just as trembling fingers gripped the soiled lip of his escape, a bellow of rage and whining roar of a friction-blade buzzing to life erupted behind him. Johnny turned his head, a tiny movement, but enough to send black spots dancing in his eyes.

The monster's one eye, bloodshot and burning with hate, fixed on the struggling escapee. A huge whirring blade, designed to carve through sheet metal, aimed with evil intent in twitching hands.

With a desperate surge, Johnny flung himself into the chute, tumbling end over end, as the pneumatic tubing shunted him through what felt like miles of pitch black tubing. Just as the new light erupted about him, Johnny found himself falling toward a wall of corpses. The glassy eyes filled his vision just before the darkness took him.

*****

Smiler whistled jauntily to himself as he walked through this little corner of the Boneyard. His secret garden, he called it. No one came here, so he didn't have to worry none. Sing-song, he talked to himself. "Takes the meat, juicy sweet. When it's done, we get some. Oh yes, dear chum!"

Picking through mounds of broken bodies and broken bits of metal in his purple suit, Smiler happened across a familiar face sitting on top of the mound. His most regular patron, Johnny C. Vid. Smiler chuckled to himself. *This day keeps getting better and better.*

The little goblin hopped over to his former customer, picking his way daintily over the juicier bits. He knelt down, chuckling to himself. "Sorry, Johnny boy. Guess your little entrepreneurial venture didn't come to much, eh chum?" No reply, though Smiler hadn't expected one. "Pity, really. Your creds were good but I know when a junkies at his limit. I can always pick 'em. And desperate enough to hit the Boneyard for a fix?" Another chortle at the former shock-jock's expense. "You really were in a bad way."

To say Smiler was surprised when Johnny reached out to snag him by the throat with a feverish strength would be an understatement. To say he shit himself in surprise when the undead Johnny raised blackened and bloodshot eyes to glare at Smiler would not be an exaggeration.

"I've seen better days," Johnny rasped out. He could barely keep his eyes open, but focused everything he had to keep his hands locked around the pusher's throat. "But I think you are gonna have an even worse one, you little carrion-eating piece of shit. Looks like you and your Pig Fucker buddy's plan didn't work." A wracking cough shook him to the core. "I'm gonna do you like he does your victims."

Smiler feebly tried to protest his innocence. "Got it all wrong! Look, I just get the left overs! Ol' Piggly Wiggly does his thing and Smiler just picks up the pieces. I'm just looking out for number one. That's the way it goes in The Heap! You know how it is, man." He scratched frantically at the vice around his neck, nails leaving bloody furrows but couldn't dislodge his former client's death-grip. "Hey, hey, Smiler's always been there for you, buddy! Let me go and I'll give ya a free hit!"

Johnny sneered at the Smiler's begging. *This must be what I looked like.* Unable to muster any more strength, he let the little worm go. Smiler scurried off as Johnny picked himself up. Slowly. Crawling down the pile of the dead, Johnny laughed. He'd never felt so alive. Being so close to death and madness had jump-started his system. When Smiler offered him the hit, he hadn't even wanted it.

I'll be sure to come back and thank you, my pig-faced friend.

Johnny intended to do exactly that... by hunting the misshapen bastard down and killing him. Thoughts of revenge kept the chill evening at bay as Johnny C. Vid, Heap dweller and former VR junkie, shuffled home to heal and plot his revenge.

DIRK DARINGMORE
and the Too-Nice Planet

Written by

Nicholas Walls

Engines screaming, a brilliant red and blue ship tore out of hyperspace, trailing scintillating bits of anti-matter behind it. At the helm, Dirk Daringmore, decorated hero of the Inter-Galactic Republic, gallantly hammered on the controls whilst screaming obscenities, quite heroically rest assured, at the top of his lungs. Helping the situation along, the recently-demoted-over-a-diplomatic-misunderstanding-but-still-hero Daringmore smashed a meaty fist against the many blinking consoles, none of which told a reassuring story. Gritting his teeth, the stalwart figure took stock of his options.

"Thrusters out, guidance computer out, weapons offline, and mini-fridge exhausted." Slamming the fridge door with a thud, the dark-haired hero gazed into his trusty dashboard mirror, steely blue eyes scanning his chiseled features. His own heroic visage never failed to bolster his flagging spirits. Nodding to himself, Dirk continued speaking to the dashing figure in the mirror. "Best to update the Captain's Log, just in case. The populace needs to know of my final heroic moments. The weeping masses, the mourning crowds... the uncertainty would cripple the Republic! The people must know!" With practiced ease from a lifetime of fisticuffs, Dirk smashed through the metal paneling and crushed the warning klaxon circuit within, its wailing ending in a choked whine. Grabbing his small battered metal microphone, Dirk Daringmore recounted his recent exploits.

"I'd stopped at Mab's Interstellar Diner for a bite to eat when my senses kicked into overdrive. Something wasn't right. Sure, it could have been the children, the nuns, or the family out for a bit of star-sighting...but I knew the culprits when I spotted some dastardly Gavlaxians up to no good!" Dirk's immaculately coiffed hair bristled at the mention of the reptilian aliens. "Sure, they SEEMED to be politely ordering a meal-to-go, but yours truly KNEW they could only be up to no good. So when those scaly freaks threatened me with some placating claw gestures and some growled threats about peace treaties and ordering food, I stood my ground and retaliated with both Ray-Guns blazing!"

Dirk shook his head at the memory. They'd been trying to convince him for years that the Gavlaxian Wars had ended. But Dirk saw through their lies.

"After that there were...complications."

Dirk's pre-emptive defense tore through one of the Gavlaxians, the meal goer behind it, and some fuel tanks behind that. Dirk was completely guiltless in the resulting chain reaction of explosions. He blamed a hitherto unknown Gavlaxian plot. Besides, the innocents of the diner would be remembered as heroes with a lovely memorial, just as soon as Dirk got back to Republic space.

"Note to self," Dirk continued into the recorder. "Look into memorial plaques when back home. And make sure to get new jacket. The old one is out of room for medals." While musing on future honors, Dirk failed to notice one of the displays urgently pinging a vibrant red.

"In my heroic escape from the exploding orbital diner, my private space craft, the *Champion*, took some shrapnel from a school-jet of nuns and children DELIBERATELY blocking my escape route. Probably enemy collaborators. Everyone knows to suspect women and children first! But not Dirk Daringmore! I am always ready for the unexpected!"

Thus it came as a bit of a surprise to the hero of the Republic when a planet rudely came into his field of vision. Caught in its gravity, the *Champion* and its pilot fell screaming toward the green and orange orb below.

The licking flames around the cockpit were only a minor cause for alarm. The sensors reading the retro thrusters malfunctioning seemed a bit concerning, and the ejection pod failing would have terrified a lesser man. But not Dirk Daringmore! Yanking on the control rod harder than the Night Queens of Edressa IV, Dirk struggled to level out the plummeting ship. Clouds and bright blue-green sky took the place of flames while below an ochre and viridian landscape rushed upwards to greet him. As the burning *Champion* leveled out, a mighty stone arc, no doubt formed by millennia of geological forces, spanned several fathoms across a canyon. Beyond the harsh rock lay a bit of scrub and a small lake. The lieutenant smirked. Not a problem. He would just thread the needle and land gracefully. Mustering skills honed through years of daring exploits, Dirk

Daringmore guided his plummeting craft toward the ancient monument and to the promised waters beyond.

It was a stupid place for a stone formation anyway. What mattered was that he had reached the little oasis. Standing beside his still steaming ship, its hull red and pinging from re-entry, the square-jawed commander surveyed the surroundings.

Beyond the small pond and its marshy surroundings, just flat lands off to the north and pristine wilderness as far as the eye could see. Which was very bad for a hero and his busted ship.

"Captain's Log continued: with amazing grace and control, I successfully managed to land my ship. Nothing stops Dirk Daringmore, not even natural law. Unfortunately, the dastardly sneak attack perpetrated by my cowardly enemies has rendered my ship unable to fly. I will explore this wild new land and see if there are any signs of life. Dirk Daringmore, signing off."

Hours later, Dirk lay collapsed in a heap in the dirt, his immaculate blue and red uniform coated in grass and dust. Two suns blazed overhead and Dirk sought shade under his jacket, heavy with medals and golden epaulettes. "Must... keep... going... for the MISSION!" Crawling forward, the hero came to an abrupt stop as a furry claw entered his blurring vision.

"I say, sir, are you quite alright?" The voice, crisp, poised, and more refined than a diplomat's daughter, came from a small hooded creature, clutching a small wooden staff in blunt little claws. Dirk's last thought before darkness claimed him was that the reaper looked smaller than he expected.

As his eyes fluttered open, Dirk immediately critiqued Heaven's décor. He lay in some kind of disgustingly comfortable bed, all white linen sheets. Light wooden paneling covered the walls, with a darker shade for the floors. The ceiling, with a softly glowing fishbowl lantern, contrasted nicely with the deep sea-green. Still, no matter how tasteful, Dirk Daringmore expected far more gold, ivory, and trumpets to greet him upon his arrival into the afterlife.

Conclusion: this must be a trap.

Closing his eyes, the wary lieutenant leaned back... and waited. He certainly didn't fall asleep. Just dozed, at most. But his keen senses alerted him to a polite knock and a door opening. Closing his eyes, he began faking snores.

"Good morning, sleepy head! The scanners tell us you should be right as rain!"

Dirk halted sawing logs and popped his head up. Before him, another one of the furred creatures stood. Dirk guessed it was about four feet tall, covered in soft fluffy fur sticking out from under blue medical scrubs. Blunt tri-claws popped out from its hands and feet. Bright, intelligent, and (ugh) friendly eyes stared out of a fuzzy, rodent-like face. It reminded Dirk of a small talking badger or otter.

As he stared at his new guest, the small badger-thing fiddled with a device in its hands and struck up a conversation.

"Well! It's a good thing we found you out there, Mr. Man! Dehydration, heat stroke, and a bit of exhaustion to boot. Quite a silly thing to go hiking in the Dust Canyons without sufficient supplies, sir. But scanners give you a clean bill of health. The doctor will be right in to check you out. Be careful in the future, okay?"

Dirk could only nod as the bubbly attendant left his room. Things were worse than he feared. He was in a MEDICAL ward. Every single scenario that ran through his head ended in "diabolical" and "torturous." Gritting his teeth, Dirk waited to meet his captor.

He didn't need to wait long. The "Doctor", as the commandant undoubtedly wished to be called, waddled in, a robust little creature wearing a white smock.

"Hello! I'm Dr. Longfellow, your physician here at Pugsterston Hospital. How are you feeling, Mr. Daringmore?"

Dirk growled through gritted teeth. "So, you know who I am." He shouldn't be surprised. His legend did span the stars.

The little badger doctor gave a hearty laugh. "Only in so much as your I.D. told me. Now, it's clear you're not from around here, what with the unique hair style." The doctor gave a pinch of his shaggy coat and a wink. "We don't get many visitors from abroad here on Yurps. What brings you to our neck of the woods?"

Dirk's mind raced as the furry thing checked him over. Sweat beaded on his head as he considered his story.

"... Fishing." Yes. A lie so blatant they couldn't possibly call him on it. Genius!

The doctor hummed distractedly. "Well, I can think of a few better places to do it. But, it's your business. Just try to stay better hydrated next time. Wouldn't want you to come on back. Now! Your clothes are in a bag by the door. Feel free to check yourself out whenever you are ready."

The badger-thing waddled over to the door.

Dirk raised a disbelieving eyebrow. "Just like that?"

The doctor chortled. "Of course! It was just a bit of heat stroke. Have a nice day!"

Dirk frowned darkly before gathering up his freshly pressed uniform. They even patched up a laser burn from the fire fight with the Mimes of Memnex. After checking his clothes for bombs, bugs, and poison but finding only a bit of spare fabric softener, the hero snuck (heroically) out of his room, hugging the hall. This house of horrors clearly doubled as a maximum security prison, as the soft yellow paint scheme made it hard to sneak around in his red and blue uniform. But valiant Dirk would not be deterred! Crouching behind a large potted fern, he warily watched the patrolling orderlies, who periodically waved at him. One even pointed him to the entrance, no doubt in fear of Dirk's famed martial prowess.

A short time later, Dirk exited the hospital. He had to give them credit; it did an excellent job hiding its true purpose as a torture chamber. The free mints at the front were particularly tasty. They had even told him where to find a good mechanic. Bracing himself for the inevitable trap, Dirk strode down the street, teeth locked in a tight grimace.

Dirk found himself exhausted again when he reached the mechanic, neon sign promising "Quality Care" in Galactic Standard. The people here were just too FRIENDLY. His arm hurt from waving hello so much and he was out of breath from the sheer volume of good mornings and how-do-you-dos.

"Fiends," Dirk gasped out.

The good times must have been part of the plan to wear him down for the real trap. Bracing himself, Dirk stepped through the turquoise painted entrance.

Inside, the smell of oil, butane, and ozone filled the air. Flashes of sparks could just be seen flaring beyond a cluttered greeting desk, past a grill gate. Mechanical parts and pieces lay in tidy piles all around, converted into tasteful furnishings for the greeting room. The whole thing had a scrappy feng shui.

A small bin, holding umbrellas and spare piping sat right by the door. No sooner did the lieutenant put foot inside, a robotic voice rasped out a dire threat. "Hello sir, welcome to our establishment! May I take your coat?" The trap had been sprung! As soon as the shiny robotic assassin lurched towards Dirk, the Republican hero swung a nearby piece of pipe with all his might. Knocking the soulless assailant off of its surprisingly knobbly legs, Dirk swung the pipe down with a thunderous crash.

"Whoa, whoa, whoa, there, friend!" Dirk whirled, pipe raised to see an overall-covered native wombat-tian approach, stubby claws waving frantically. "Sorry, buddy, didn't realize you were an Android-phobic. Ol' Brassknob there was just trying to be polite."

Dirk looked down at the dented robot. It was indeed merely an aging butler droid, one of thousands across the stars. Only with a large dent in the front of its black matte chassis. Its cerulean monocle-optic clicked and whirred as it looked up at the immaculately coiffed assailant.

"Terribly sorry about the misunderstanding, sir. I seem to have fallen down."

Dirk dropped the pipe and whistled innocently, looking at everything except the fallen droid. A moment of shuffling, apologies, and hefting later, the mechanic had worked the brass 'bot upright.

"Now then, with all the commotion out of the way, introductions are in order. My name is Stoderric. You can call me Stod. What brings you to my shop?"

Dirk cleared his throat and began in the same voice he used to impress recruits and seduce news reporters with alliterative names. "Well, citizen, I am Dirk Daringmore. My ship is badly damaged and in need of repair. I am on an urgent mission for the Republic and it is imperative I am on my way as soon as possible."

Stod typed away on a hand-held pad, much like the nurses. "Yep. Rush job. Work related. And what is the make and model of your vehicle?"

Dirk cocked his head, disturbed by the little creature's stoic response. The lieutenant expected any good red-blooded life-form to be greatly roused after such a stirring example of rhetoric. Dirk had led platoons of men to their valorous deaths with such speeches! Suspicions of treachery flared again as Dirk glared at Stod.

"*Traveler* class, luxury model, with upgraded Hyperdrive Charger. '09 model. M-Class."

The diminutive mechanic let out an impressed whistle. Dirk wondered how that worked, what with the muzzle and all. "Nice one. Classic. And where is it parked?"

"Ummm, parked?"

"Right, parked. I'm going to have to send one of my girls out to pick it up and bring it in."

The stranded hero's hands flapped somewhat uselessly in the air, as though groping for the right words. "You see, it's... back that way." He pointed absently toward a wall. "Out in the wastes."

Stod paused and looked up from his pad, gave Dirk a once over, then....reached out and patted the hero on the shoulder. Though he did have to stand on a nearby crate to do it.

"Crashed it, did you? Well, say no more! Explains why you took a stick to Brassknob, too. Being all shook up like that! You just relax and we will fix you up right as rain!" Quick as a flash, Stod lost his sympathetic mien and was all business, barking orders as loudly and efficiently as any drill sergeant in the Republic military.

The day passed in a blur as the little mechanics dragged in his beloved *Champion* by hover-tug, stripped her down, and put the ship back together in record time. Meanwhile, Dirk enjoyed complimentary hot drinks and, after testing it for poisons, found it to be absolutely delicious. The final straw came as he boarded his ship. Stod handed him a slip of sheet paper.

"Don't worry about the bill. We have a policy of lending a helping hand here on Yurps. If you ever come this way again, we can settle up accounts then. Maybe you can help someone else get out of a sticky situation."

As they bid him a fond farewell, Dirk resolved then and there to return to Yurps. At the head of a full battle-fleet. NO ONE could be that nice! It must be a cover for something diabolical and sinister. It was the only logical explanation. As the *Champion* broke orbit around Yurps and set course for home, Dirk turned on his trusty recorder.

"Captain's Log continued: after salvaging my ship single-handedly, alone, and without aid, I have uncovered what may be the most vile den of savagery and villainy in the known universe..."

Dirk Daringmore, Hero of the Inter-Galactic Republic, set off for home.

Tears of Stone

Written by

K.N. Nguyen

I

The fire crackled merrily in the hearth as Norbryn tossed another log in. Brightly-colored baubles decorated the hearth and mantle, while crisp, green leaves and gaudy red berries adorned the door frames. A single geode containing emerald crystals took command of the center of the mantle in memory of the ancestors who had passed on.

Children giggled as Morgance brought in a plate of sweetbread for the family to enjoy. Each child greedily grabbed a piece of sweetbread and stuffed it eagerly into their mouths. Norbryn chuckled at his children's chipmunk cheeks full of the rich pastry. LaRaaz'n, the oldest child at the age of fourteen, tried to at least appear dignified with his chipmunk cheeks bulging. Yuri and Xan'ni, the nine-year-old twins, laughed through their stuffed mouths, spraying crumbs at their mother and father.

"Come on, you little monsters," Morgance playfully chided, "It's time for bed. You know that the spirit of the winter solstice won't visit if you're all awake." Wagging a finger knowingly at her children, Morgance said in her lovely, sing-song voice, "You'll get no gifts at this rate."

Cries rang out from LaRaaz'n and his sisters as they quickly swallowed their sweetbread to protest. This caused another bout of laughter from Norbryn. "Off to bed with you then," he urged, shooing his children towards their rooms. LaRaaz'n attempted to act aloof, but he was quickly caught up in his father's infectious energy and joined his sisters in darting to their rooms. As soon as the children were in their beds and their bedroom doors closed, Norbryn wrapped his wife in a tight embrace. "Shall we enjoy some of this year's festivities?" he murmured in her ear.

Arching her back against his thick hands, Morgance shot her husband an alluring smile. The two shared a deep, passionate kiss. Pulling away slightly, Morgance reached around Norbryn and grabbed a piece of sweetbread. "Bryn, do you think that the children will be happy with this year's gifts? King Colgar's taxes have been so unreasonable this past year. We've barely scraped by."

"We've managed before and we'll manage again," Norbryn said, soothingly. "Once King Colgar gets over his obsession with capturing all of the 'witches' in Mithrandar, he'll finally return the tax rate to what it used to be." Norbryn boasted the title of the land's top five apothecaries. His knowledge of the medicinal processes of herbs and their efficacy when mixed with other herbs was rivaled by none, causing him to be labeled as the best apothecary by some. Through his apothecary work, he was able to provide for the family.

With the increase of taxes, Morgance had to take on a job as a seamstress to keep their family afloat. Despite the heavy taxation, Norbryn did not compromise his integrity or the health of his patients by using low quality herbs or cheap substitutes. "Besides, LaRaaz'n has been unbelievably helpful in keeping an eye on his sisters. I even saw him working as an apprentice to Grant, the physician, lately," he soothed.

Allowing herself to be lost in Norbryn's strong embrace once more, Morgance tried to relax. A bright flash of light caught their eyes followed by a low rumbling roar in the distance. Releasing his wife and walking over to the window, Norbryn looked into the darkness. A light layer of white powder had started to build on the windowsill. Darkness engulfed their sleepy little town. The only source of light came from the dancing flames of the hearth reflected in the window. Norbryn walked back towards his wife. "I wonder what that was."

The two grabbed another piece of sweetbread and started to nibble on it in uneasy silence. Without warning, a siren blared to life in their town. Its shrill tone caused LaRaaz'n, Yuri, and Xan'ni to rush from their rooms into the family room, hands clasped tightly on their ears.

"Father, what's going on?" LaRaaz'n cried out.

Before Norbryn could answer, an explosion tore the house apart as one of the King's explosives was dropped on their home. Splinters of wood and chunks of stone were blasted apart and crashed into neighboring homes. The fire in the hearth roared into a blaze that rivaled the seven hells and set several homes on fire. Briefly, Norbryn watched his family fly in several directions before smashing his head on the stone base of a neighboring house before succumbing to darkness.

II

The explosion reverberated through young LaRaaz'n and struck him to the core. His body thrown violently into the air. He landed twenty feet from his family's living room, head smacking against the ground. Stars burst in his field of vision as he struggled to maintain consciousness. Heat from the surrounding fire threatened to burn his flesh, its flames moving ever closer in hopes of licking his young skin. A sharp pain briefly blossomed on his left shoulder before his body was almost instantly relaxed. Blood dripped into his eyes from a gash in his forehead.

Struggling to prop himself up on his elbow, LaRaaz'n's vision swam with the effort. It took every bit of effort for him to steady himself on his elbow. After a few minutes, his vision cleared and he was able to observe the destroyed homes in his quiet little town. Fifteen homes were destroyed by several explosions while others were being consumed by flames. Bodies lay strewn amongst the rubble. Some did not move. Others were slowly trying to move their limbs as they either regained consciousness or tested for broken limbs. Many were running either from the rubble and flames, or towards it.

Through the hazy smoke, the figure of a lone woman made her way through the bodies. She stopped at each body and examined it. Some she would lay back on the ground, presumably a corpse. Others she would attempt to help to their feet or offer a few inaudible words of comfort. As she made her way towards him, LaRaaz'n noticed that she was not spending too long at any one individual. LaRaaz'n tried to push himself up with both arms, but a sudden pain shot through his left shoulder and down his arm, causing him to cry out in agony. His cry alerted the woman and drew her towards him.

As soon as she neared him, she kneeled down and inspected him. Pulling the left sleeve of his nightshirt up, she let out a small gasp. Staring at his shoulder, she reached out and tenderly touched his wound. LaRaaz'n grimaced in pain at her touch. Picking LaRaaz'n's body up in her surprisingly strong arms, she quickly started to walk out of the blazing town.

Bodies lay littered on the ground. LaRaaz'n vaguely recognized his mother and two sisters. Morgance's arms were splayed at unnatural angles and the twins were slumped together by the brightly-colored baubles that had once adorned the living room. La'Raaz'n's eyes watered slightly. Seeing the prone bodies of his family coupled with the gently growing pain in his left shoulder threatened to overwhelm him. Forcing himself to ignore his anguish, LaRaaz'n tried to focus on clearing his vision and studying the woman who carried him away from his home.

This close in the darkness, he noticed that she wore a light blouse, even in the chilly winter air. Over the blouse, a leather coat with fur lining the collar and sleeves. Her hair framed a heart-shaped face. On the right side of her face, something protruded from her cheeks. Even though he squinted his eyes, LaRaaz'n could not make out what jutted from her face. His vision continued to swim, threatening to overwhelm him. Finally, as they left the town and entered the woods LaRaaz'n succumbed to his injuries and blacked out.

*****

Slowly, LaRaaz'n opened his eyes. His body was pleasantly warm and the pain in his head was receding. He struggled to sit up, but his left arm would not support his weight while fully bandaged from his shoulder down to his elbow. A gasp of pain escaped him as he quickly lowered himself onto his back once more.

"Careful now," a cool female voice chided. "You've received a serious injury on your shoulder that'll take a good length of time to heal."

"It doesn't hurt much though," LaRaaz'n complained.

Moving into the light of the fire, the woman stared at LaRaaz'n and clucked her tongue. "Och, you're quite the strong one, aren't you?" In the light, LaRaaz'n was able to fully make out her features. Her strawberry blonde hair framed her face. She had the youthful look that those who were blessed with a baby face could only enjoy. He could see the pale, purple stones that marred her otherwise lovely face. Noticing his gaze, she reached up and gently touched the stones. "Amethyst. I must say, your emeralds are lovely."

"Emeralds?" LaRaaz'n asked. "What are you talking about? Why do you have amethyst in your face? Who are you?"

A tinkling chuckle rang forth from her naturally rosy lips. "My name is Bronwyn. Och, you ask a lot of questions." As she started answering the rest of his questions, her face became somber and her eyes looked inwards. "Have you heard of King Colgar's desire to wipe out the Spliced?" LaRaaz'n shook his head. "People who are Spliced are people who have stones or crystals embedded in their flesh." She pointed to the amethyst in her cheek.

"The King believes people like us are a danger to him." LaRaaz'n opened his mouth to ask a question, but Bronwyn held up a hand to silence him. "Those who are Spliced can utilize the energies in their stones to do feats that some would call magic. What people don't understand is that every time energy is drawn from the stones, the stones dissolve and shorten the life of the Spliced. If a Spliced person were to use all of their energy, the stone would disappear and the Spliced would die."

LaRaaz'n's eyes widened in horror at this revelation. "How does this affect me?"

Bronwyn smiled gently at LaRaaz'n. "You have become Spliced." She pointed to his bandaged shoulder. "My guess would be that a geode connected with you during the bombings. Tell me, what is your name?"

"LaRaaz'n. Where is my family? Are they...?" His voice trailed off, unable to complete the frightening thought.

"Your family is no longer a part of your life. You may live with me, if you like. I can help you come to understand your new gifts."

LaRaaz'n stared into the hearth, heartbroken at the thought of never seeing his family again. The silence stretched for several minutes. Slowly, LaRaaz'n took a deep breath and forced himself to move forward. "How did you become Spliced?"

A dark shadow crossed Bronwyn's eyes briefly, but she answered his question without hesitation. "I used to work as a linguistics tutor for the King and his son. Prince Luther was well-known amongst the female servants for his lecherous behavior. One day, he turned his attentions to me." Her voice softened and the shadow crossed her eyes once more.

"I don't understand," LaRaaz'n said. "Did he shoot amethyst stones from his eyes into your face?"

A wan smile tugged at Bronwyn's lips at his innocence. "Prince Luther attempted to have his way with me. He gained the upper hand and had me pinned on the ground. I struggled to break free and dug my nails deep into his face. I almost gouged his eyes out. After I did that, he grabbed a geode from a nearby table and smashed it against my face." Waving her hand towards the amethyst once more, Bronwyn finished weakly, "The results are that I became Spliced. Isn't it interesting that the king fears the Spliced, yet he insists that every home keeps at least one geode in honor of His Majesty?" She chuckled once more at her musings. Her laugh was like the tinkling of a bell. LaRaaz'n longed to listen to Bronwyn laugh again.

"I'm sorry that he did that to you. Do they know what they did to you? That you're... Spliced?" LaRaaz'n's eyes held a deep sorrow as he digested everything Bronwyn told him.

Reaching out and touching LaRaaz'n's face gently, Bronwyn smiled softly and said, "I don't think they do. All the same, I'd rather not announce my condition to the world." She winked at LaRaaz'n playfully.

The sparkle in her eyes calmed LaRaaz'n and eased his concerns. As he started to relax a little bit, he noticed for the first time he was ravenous. "Is there anything to eat? How long was I unconscious?"

"You were out for almost a day. I've got some eggs, sausages, and potatoes that I can heat up for you. However, while you wait, I think I can scrounge up something for you. Give me a moment." Bronwyn headed out of the room. After rummaging in the kitchen briefly, she returned with a warm butter cookie. Handing it to LaRaaz'n, she propped him up on a pillow before heading back into the kitchen to warm up his meal.

LaRaaz'n took a bite of the cookie. Its buttery flavor exploded in his mouth. He swallowed and took another bite, savoring its delicious taste. Once he consumed the cookie, LaRaaz'n gingerly touched his bandages with his right hand. Rubbing his fingers over the wound, he felt the protruding presence of the geode crystals in his shoulder. There were roughly five crystals embedded in his shoulder and they barely stuck out more than an inch from his flesh. He noted that the back of his hand had many small scrapes where debris had struck it.

Bronwyn returned carrying a plate piled with scrambled eggs, sausages, and seasoned roasted potatoes. Setting the plate down on the floor, she went into the kitchen and returned with a glass of water. "Eat up," she instructed. "If you need any more, I can get it."

LaRaaz'n dug into the meal with the ravenous enthusiasm of a starving wolf. Bronwyn sat near him, occasionally watching LaRaaz'n with an amused expression as he devoured his food. A third of the way into his meal, LaRaaz'n started to slow down. Chewing thoughtfully, LaRaaz'n turned to Bronwyn and swallowed. "Why exactly does the King insist that we keep geodes in our homes if he fears the Spliced so much? Why does he even fear them?"

"He fears us because we are able to metabolize the crystals in our body and use the energy that is created to do some spectacular things. One of the most famous Spliced has become known only as 'Celeste' because of her celestite crystals."

"I've never heard of anyone in our annals named Celeste," LaRaaz'n said between bites.

"The Caileanach family has done a good job of hiding the Spliced from history and creating a false trail to cover up their search. Colgar's witch hunt is no more than him feigning a belief in malicious spirits to make sure that no one notices he is secretly finding and destroying our numbers.

"Celeste fought alongside King Alasdair against the Lothan Empire, ultimately freeing our people and allowing us to create the land of Mithrandar. She displayed spectacular power and drew the eye of the King. After the battle, she was severely weakened due to the amount of energy she used in the battle. Alasdair saw that, and ordered her capture and execution. When the few Spliced and their friends cried out against the injustice, he then began his persecution of the Spliced. This persecution has been passed down for over two centuries and is continued by Colgar. They require us to keep the geodes in our homes to honor Celeste's contribution to the formation of Mithrandar. I've always found it to be a twisted way to pay respect to a woman who not only freed us, but died because of it."

LaRaaz'n stared at Bronwyn in disbelief. A bit of egg dangled from his fork, forgotten on its way to his mouth. "That is unbelievable! So they've basically wiped the Spliced out since Celeste?"

"Not exactly," Bronwyn explained. "It is very rare to become Spliced. Only extremely traumatic events, like an explosion or sudden, forceful contact, cause the geodes to become embedded in the skin. Many people, once they discovered that they were Spliced, did not last very long. They used up their life energies trying to overthrow the Caileanach line. Others just went into hiding. Besides us, the only two others that I know of are Agate and Quartz. Agate is actually a friend of Celeste's and has managed to stay out of the royals' sights for two hundred fifty years. I met Quartz a few years ago after I became Spliced and she was pretty freshly Spliced herself. We can meet them once you've healed and learned to control your gifts."

"I would like that. Can we also visit my town, Uran?"

"I'm sorry, but no we can't. It was destroyed in the King's explosion. I doubt that anyone will be there by the time you're well enough to travel."

"I see," LaRaaz'n said.

Placing a hand on his right shoulder, Bronwyn gave him a slight squeeze. "Things will be all right. I promise."

III

LaRaaz'n hung back near the outskirts of the town of Loam. At seventeen, he grew a couple feet taller and his body had hardened after years of physical training. He wore a loose, tan tunic over black trousers. His shoulder had healed, but the loose tunic hid the jagged emerald crystals embedded in his left shoulder. Taking a deep breath, he stepped out from the tree-line and made his way into the town. Though no one would know him or what he was, LaRaaz'n felt as though eyes followed him throughout the town. He walked into a butcher's shop and mulled over the meats.

"How can I help ye, me boy?" the jovial butcher asked. He had a portly figure with a balding head. He grabbed a rag and wiped his hands off.

LaRaaz'n stared at the juicy cuts of meat hanging from the ceiling, unable to make up his mind. "The lamb and goat both look good. How about some of each?"

The butcher went off and pulled down a lamb carcass and portioned off a richly marbled piece. Wrapping up the meat, he secured the paper and then busied himself with cutting out a choice piece of goat for LaRaaz'n. LaRaaz'n continued to make his way around the shop, looking at the various meats. His mind wandered. It had been almost three years since he dared set foot in one of the neighboring towns after the bombing of his hometown. During those three years, he had spent countless hours with Bronwyn, practicing not only martial combat, but how to safely tap into the energy of the emeralds that fused within his body and how to manipulate that energy. In that time, he had grown close to Bronwyn. She had not only been his mentor, but she had worked her way into his soul.

"All set, me boy," the butcher said, startling him from his reverie. "That'll be two gold and seven silvers." He held out his fleshy hand for his coins.

LaRaaz'n reached into his pocket and pulled out the coins, dropping them into the man's hand. He gathered his purchases and walked out of the store with a word of thanks. Holding the packages at his side, LaRaaz'n made his way through the town towards the baker's shop. Today would be a day to remember—he was determined to make it so. Upon reaching the bakery, he stopped outside to stare at the fresh pastries in the window. His eyes fell on the creampuffs with fresh strawberries adorning the top, and he knew instantly that this was what he needed. Entering the store, he quickly purchased two creampuffs and exited, his shopping completed.

As he walked through the streets of the town, LaRaaz'n thought about what it took to make himself invisible: a shadow walking through the light. Observe the surroundings and adapt your demeanor accordingly. In a town like Loam, all he needed to do was take on an air of leisure on this beautiful, sunny day. Neighbors walked around and chatted pleasantly with each other. Not a frown or stern look could be found. LaRaaz'n incorporated this into his physiology as he strolled out of Loam. He smiled at a lovely, young woman carrying a basket of flowers. Her flaxen hair was tied in a loose ponytail and hung over her right shoulder. A handful of children ran past him after a scruffy dog, laughing and calling out to each other.

In no time at all, LaRaaz'n made his way out of Loam and into the woods. As he entered the quiet of the woods, his apprehension started to melt away and excitement filled him. He walked quickly back to Bronwyn's small cottage outside of Uran. Lavender and orange flowers bloomed along the path. LaRaaz'n stooped over and picked several blooms. He entered the cottage and placed the meats and pastries on the kitchen counter. Grabbing a glass, he filled it partway with water and put the flowers inside. He placed the glass on a table by the window and went back into the kitchen to prepare dinner.

LaRaaz'n chopped the carrots, potatoes, and onions and placed them in a pan on the stove. After seasoning the lamb and goat, he placed the meats into the sizzling pan with the vegetables. The juicy scent of meat coupled with the vegetables and spices filled the cottage and made his stomach growl. As he plated the meal, LaRaaz'n heard the front door unlock and open. Turning away from the plates, he watched as Bronwyn closed the door and locked it. "Welcome home, Bron," he called out cheerily.

Bronwyn turned away from the door and LaRaaz'n noticed that her eyes were red and puffy. As she looked at LaRaaz'n, she broke down and began to cry. LaRaaz'n rushed to her side and grabbed her tightly. He held her as she cried into his good shoulder. "What's wrong, Bron?"

"They found Quartz," Bronwyn replied, gasping between sobs. "She's dead." She then fell silent as she wept. Her hand grabbed at his tunic and bunched it up.

LaRaaz'n continued to hold her tenderly, all thoughts of dinner forgotten. His hand gently cupped the back of her head as her warm tears pooled onto his shoulder. "Everything will be all right," he murmured. "I'll keep you safe."

*****

Bronwyn awoke the next morning in her bed. Her comforter rested gently against her chin. The morning light shone softly through her curtains, warming the room. Looking around, she noticed her bedroom door was open and LaRaaz'n's bedroll looked as though it had not been slept in. Bronwyn slid out of bed and walked towards the door. Opening it a crack, Bronwyn noticed that LaRaaz'n lay sleeping in one of the chairs at the dining room table. On the table was a glass filled with lavender and orange flowers. Their light scent filled the room. She hadn't noticed them yesterday in her grief.

Shuffling into the kitchen, Bronwyn noticed that there was small brown package tied with a cord. She opened the box and inside was two melting creampuffs. The strawberries on top were starting to turn a light brown around the edges and the cream leaked out of the sides of the creampuffs. A slight groan alerted her to LaRaaz'n, who began to stir. Picking up the box, Bronwyn opened the window to throw the spoiled pastry to the wolfhounds that roamed the woods. She noticed scraps of meat that had not been fully eaten from the night before. Her heart skipped a beat as she dropped the creampuffs out the window.

"Morning, Bron," LaRaaz'n said groggily. "How are you feeling?"

"All right, I suppose," her voice was heavy and hoarse from the lack of hydration the night before. "Did you stay out here all night?"

"Yeah, I didn't want to wake you once you fell asleep."

"Would you like to go out for breakfast?" she asked.

Stretching lazily, LaRaaz'n shook his head. "I'll bring something back for us. You go and relax." He smiled a tired smile as he got up stiffly from the chair.

Bronwyn walked over to LaRaaz'n and gently touched his face. "Did you prepare something for us last night?"

Suppressing a yawn, LaRaaz'n nodded his head. He quickly tried to stifle another yawn as he noticed Bronwyn's eyes had started to water. "It's okay, Bron," he hurriedly added. "I saved what I could for later today." He rested his hand on her shoulder and gently began rubbing her back. "Last night was a hard one for both of us."

Bronwyn leaned into LaRaaz'n and took a deep breath. A subtle aroma of seasoned lamb and goat clung to him. He must have made it for dinner last night. LaRaaz'n knew that lamb was her favorite. He also knew that she loved fresh strawberries. Taking another deep breath, Bronwyn reached up and wrapped her arms around him. She leaned her head into his chest and felt his hand cup the back of her head. His fingers wrapped into her hair and she felt his body quiver, ever so slightly. Bronwyn looked up at LaRaaz'n and stared into his eyes.

His eyes still held the innocence of youth, despite everything he had gone through in the last three years. Staring deep into the clear blue pools of his eyes, she also noted the longing that lay below the surface. As she gazed into his longing, Bronwyn felt a twinge of guilt as she recognized the look. She reached out and tentatively grabbed his hand. He did not pull away from her. Bronwyn reversed her grip on his hand and pulled out of his embrace. With a coy look in her eye, she led him back to her room. Bronwyn watched his eyes widen in surprise before a look of desire filled them. She had seen that desire flash in his eyes on several occasions throughout the years, but tried to ignore it. Today, she would not ignore it.

LaRaaz'n could not mask his excitement as Bronwyn pulled him into her room. He stopped automatically at the foot of her bed. She climbed onto her bed and laid down on her side. Her eyes beckoned him to join her. Her body cried out for physical comfort, however, there was no grief or doubt in her eyes. Hesitantly, he crawled onto her bed and wrapped his arms around her. The two shared a deep kiss. LaRaaz'n's hand slid under her tunic and cupped her back in his hand. Bronwyn wrapped her hand into his hair and pulled him closer to her. Her body pressed against his, begging for his touch, and he happily obliged.

IV

Bronwyn and LaRaaz'n made their way to Ryder, a town five miles west of Uran. It had been four years since Bronwyn had found out about Quartz's death. The two had grown close since the day after they found out the horrible news. As they neared the town, they saw that the Spring Festival was in full swing. Bouquets of flowers adorned everything from the posts that held the torches to the gates that surrounded the town, and were woven in the hair of every female. Girls pranced about in brightly-colored sundresses, their hair dancing about their shoulders in soft ringlets or cascading waves. Boys darted about the town, either chasing the young girls or shaggy-haired dogs.

LaRaaz'n, now twenty-one, wore a soft yellow tunic with brown trousers. Though it was lightly colored, it hid his emerald crystals completely. Bronwyn wore a pale pink dress with matching wildflowers braided in her strawberry blonde hair. The amethyst crystals on her face were covered by her hair that she draped over the left side, partially hiding her eye. "I haven't seen a festival like this in ages," LaRaaz'n breathed. "I forgot how happy people could be."

"Shall we?" Bronwyn asked, extending her hand.

LaRaaz'n smiled a large, boyish grin and took her hand. Together, the two entered Ryder and joined in the festivities. People called out to each other and waved as they walked through the town. The tension that had lined the eyes of the parents and elders for the last seven years had softened and their smiles were genuine. The worry remained, but today they were able to relax, if only a little. There hadn't been any bombings in the last three years and that was a reason to hope that the darker days were behind them. No one paid much attention to the two. Greetings were called out to them and they were returned with good cheer. Throughout it all, the musical sound of laughter filled the air.

At the heart of the town there was a large wooden may pole with a rainbow of ribbons. Girls and young women began choosing a color as a group of fiddlers set up by the pole. Once all of the ribbons found a hand to rest in, the fiddlers struck a cheery tempo and began sawing away. The may pole participants started to dance around the pole. They wove in between each other, covering the pole in a beautiful braid. LaRaaz'n watched the dance with rapt attention.

Bronwyn slipped away and started talking to a woman with a burnt face further away. Returning his attention to the dancing women, two of them caught his attention. Chestnut hair that rested halfway down their backs, cheeks lightly dusted with freckles, and identical dimples that appeared by the corners of their mouths as they smiled and laughed with their friends. LaRaaz'n's heart dropped and rage quickly filled him as he recognized his little sisters, Yuri and Xa'ni. Time had been very kind to them for they had grown into lovely young ladies.

Quickly finding Bronwyn once more, he recognized the woman that she spoke with. Morgance's face bore the shiny scar of a burn, but she was just as LaRaaz'n remembered her on that fateful winter's eve. Scanning the crowd, LaRaaz'n's eye caught the gaze of one of the fiddlers. Norbryn's right eye grew wide in surprise as he saw his son for the first time in seven years. His left eye had been lost in the explosion, but its absence did not take away from the pain that filled his face.

LaRaaz'n turned and stormed towards the town gate. Bronwyn, noticing LaRaaz'n's sudden movement, broke away from Morgance and hastily tried to follow him. "LaRaaz'n!" She called out. "Wait!"

LaRaaz'n rounded on her. Anger filled his face and it took all of his self-control to not shout at her. "You lied to me!" he hissed. "How could you tell me that my family was dead? Why did you keep them from me?"

"I never told you they were dead," Bronwyn said, her voice pained. "I told you that they were no longer part of your life. Once you became Spliced, you not only put yourself in danger, but your family as well. If you went back to live with your family, they would've found you and killed your entire family like they did Quartz." LaRaaz'n's eyes softened slightly, but he did not let go of the anger that coursed through him.

"You kept me from them while you carried on a relationship with my parents," he accused.

"It's true," she admitted. "I've been in contact with them the whole time. I've been telling them about you, and the man you've become." Bronwyn attempted a wan smile, but the tears that started welling up at the corner of her eyes did not have the desired, soothing effect. "Please," she begged, "you must understand that I did what was best for everyone. Your parents asked that I keep you safe when I went back to Uran on the night of the bombing after I rescued you."

LaRaaz'n unable to contain his rage, stormed off into the woods. As he made his way into the woods, he heard Bronwyn's mournful cry as she begged him to come back.

LaRaaz'n stomped through the woods, his blood boiling as he imagined his parents abandoning him, never coming to look for him. How could they do this to me? LaRaaz'n snapped a low hanging branch that dared to be in his path. Stopping suddenly, LaRaaz'n took a deep breath and took stock of his surroundings. He had wandered onto a worn dirt path. Up ahead, he noticed the roof of a chapel, indicating that a town was nearby.

LaRaaz'n started to make his way away from the town when a deafening explosion destroyed the chapel in a ball of flame. Screams and panicked cries rent the air. Without thinking, LaRaaz'n started running towards the burning town. As he entered the town, a second explosion on the far end of the town almost knocked him off of his feet. Debris flew everywhere. A sudden searing pain in his left side caught his attention. A large piece of glass stuck out of his side and had buried itself deep into his body.

With a grunt of pain, LaRaaz'n pulled the glass out of his side. Blood flowed out of the wound, pooling onto his tunic. The pain was so intense that his head started to spin. Taking a deep breath, LaRaaz'n concentrated on healing himself. As he focused on his thoughts, his skin started to knit itself together, closing the wound and preventing any infection that may have occurred. Sweat beaded on his forehead at the effort. After he finished healing himself, LaRaaz'n brought his hand to his shoulder to feel his emerald crystals. One of his five crystals could no longer be found. He'd used it up completely. Four remained.

LaRaaz'n tore his mind from the missing crystal, the lost life energy, and started running through the town once more. Flames poured from windows and on the roofs of houses. People called out to their loved ones. Others tried to tend to the wounded, covering gashes and trying to cool burns. Children cried out for their mothers. Chickens squawked, cows lowed, and horses whinnied. The town was in complete chaos. LaRaaz'n turned a corner and heard the quiet whimper of a young child. Turning to his right, he noticed a toddler, no more than a year old with flaming red hair and covered in freckles, hiding behind a barrel. She seemed to have escaped the devastating damage of the explosions.

Without thinking, LaRaaz'n grabbed the girl into his arms and started running through the town trying to find her parents. No one paid him any heed or noticed the girl in his arms. After searching for several minutes, LaRaaz'n noticed uniformed soldiers wearing the King's emblem had started to enter the town, weapons drawn. As swiftly as he could, LaRaaz'n turned and made his way to back into the woods.

As he left the burning town behind, LaRaaz'n hefted the young girl in his arms. She hadn't cried at all during the whole ordeal. Her emerald eyes were filled with fear, but they remained dry. LaRaaz'n made his way through the woods back towards Ryder.

Before he reached Ryder, LaRaaz'n saw Bronwyn making her way towards him. "LaRaaz'n! Where did you go?" Noticing the child, Bronwyn's face grew concerned. "Who is this?" Once she reached him, she smiled sweetly at the little girl and grabbed her chubby fist.

"I don't know," he replied. "Her town was bombed and then the King's men arrived. I left before they could see me."

"Och, is that so?" Bronwyn said in a high pitched voice. Her attention was on the child. LaRaaz'n watched as the fear slowly left the girl's eyes and curiosity replaced it.

"Bron, we can't take her back... can we?"

Not taking her eyes off of the child, Bronwyn shook her head. "I'm afraid not. They will have bombed that town for a reason. Possibly they thought that a Spliced was hiding there. If we bring her back, they will lock her up. They have no regard for even the innocent."

LaRaaz'n absorbed her words. After a lengthy pause, he asked, "Is this what you had to deal with when you pulled me from Uran?"

At last, Bronwyn faced him. "If I would've treated you and returned you to your parents, you all would be dead. I did what was best for everyone. They gave their blessing."

LaRaaz'n watched the little girl smile as Bronwyn made silly faces at her. "I want to save her like you saved me. Will you help?"

"Of course," Bronwyn said with a smile. The two made their way back to their home, the little girl bouncing lightly in LaRaaz'n's arms. "What should we name her?" she asked.

LaRaaz'n thought for a while. "How about Aranwen, after my grandmother?"

"That's a lovely name."

The three entered the home and shut the door behind them. LaRaaz'n set little Aranwen on their bed in Bronwyn's room. Almost instantly, she lay down on the bed and closed her eyes. Aranwen was asleep in moments.

LaRaaz'n brushed a strand of hair off of her freckled face. A gentle smile filled his face. Today had been a great day for the Spring Festival. Despite the tragedy earlier at that unknown town, LaRaaz'n finally felt at peace when he thought of his family. His parents and sisters were alive, Bronwyn was still here with him, and now he had a daughter. Bronwyn made her way into the room and put a hand on his back. The two looked at each other and smiled. Their little family was growing.

Windstrider

Written by

K.N. Nguyen

I

Freyna danced merrily as she rode the ever-shifting air currents. Her periwinkle hair blew softly behind her as she twirled and leapt about. Eyes closed, she imagined that she floated like a leaf. Skin as pale as a cirrocumulus cloud and eyes like obsidian. Freyna's petite frame made her look smaller and fragile, belying her true strength. Although she looked no older than an eight-year-old, she had the force of the Wind at her command. Today, however, she was a leaf, riding the eddies and currents through the heavens.

"Freyna!" the stern, rumbling voice of her oldest brother rang out. Her eyes snapped open at his call. "Come over for a moment, will you?"

Freyna skipped lightly towards her brother in the main hall, still spinning and twirling since she was, after all, a leaf. "Yes, Graak?" She closed her eyes once more and began dancing again. The spacious room of the main hall sparkled as the crystalline structures reflected the rays of the morning sun in the skies.

Suppressing a smile on his usually solemn face, Graak tried to maintain a level of composure. With his little sister around, it wasn't always easy to keep a stern demeanor. Graak's body, the dark black-grey of the storm clouds, lay hidden behind wisps of heavy storm clouds and tornadoes while his temper fluctuated like the sudden summer storms. When he became angry, the clouds started to roil and expand from his body. Today, they gently spread from his torso and limbs. As the eldest brother, he took it upon himself to make sure that Freyna and their brother, Thuul, did not accidentally wreak havoc on the people of the world. "How would you like to go down to dance in the wheat fields of Rydier for a while and then play in the Silver Sea for a bit? It's getting too stale down there and the people could use a cooling breeze."

Waving her arms around her like a ballerina, Freyna closed her eyes once more and asked, "Can I stay for two days? There's a village in the mountains that I want to visit."

"No, two days is too long for you to go on your own."

Entering the main hall, Thuul teased his older brother, "Come now, Graak, she's old enough by now to spend two days among the humans." The middle child, Thuul had an athletic figure that was a pale grey, like the clouds just before a light spring storm. Like his brother, wisps of clouds emanated from his body. Unlike his brother, they only entangled themselves in his hair.

"She's too young," Graak said with a slight edge in his voice. His deep timbre sounded very much like thunder.

"Freyna needs to experience the world. You can't coddle her forever." Thuul replied, steady and light-hearted as a spring storm.

Throughout it all, Freyna continued to dance and started circling her brothers. Her eyes were closed and her visage serene as the two argued about her. "Thuul was younger than me when he started spending time amongst the humans, wasn't he?" Her voice held no tone of accusation, nor any strong interest in the matter at hand. "If he could do it, why can't I? I want to visit that village and if I'm in Rydier and the Silver Sea, I'll not have time to check it out."

Thuul smiled at Graak as his brother worked to come up with a compelling reason to keep their little sister from spending too much time down with Man. "I suppose that you are old enough by now," Graak said slowly. "I want you back before sunset on the second day."

Opening her eyes as she spun, Freyna's face remained relaxed. "As you say." Running her hands through her hair briefly, she smoothed it out before diving down to the earth. She tumbled gracefully down to the ground and made her way to the wheat fields of Rydier. Her white dress flapped softly around her during her descent. The fields were bursting with grain. The air around her was pleasantly warm, but it felt a bit stale. Farmers dabbed their faces with handkerchiefs or the back of their hands. Taking a deep breath, Freyna jumped into the air and began to dance slowly through the fields. Stalks gently bent as she moved amongst them. Farmers smiled at the welcomed relief that her breeze brought. In the distance, a cow bellowed, wanting to be milked. Refreshed, one of the farmers made his way towards the barn to milk the cow.

After providing the farmers with a cooling zephyr, Freyna made her way through the land and to the Silver Sea, satisfied with her work. She watched as the waves gently rolled upon the white sand beach, breaking slightly and lapping against the large stones. Giggling, Freyna dove down to the sea and skimmed her toes over the cool waters. A salty spray lightly splashed her face. Banking a sharp curve, Freyna headed out towards the open waters and then spun to return to the shore. Waves crashed against the large rocks, causing the sunbathing seals to dive into the waters. The pups started chasing each other and diving in between the waves. In the distance, a small pod of dolphins could be seen jumping out of the waters.

A seal pup came up to Freyna's side and gently nuzzled her bare feet. Spinning in the air until she was upside down, Freyna dangled her arms above the pup's head and rubbed it like a child would scratch a dog or cat behind the ears. The seal closed its eyes in contentment at her touch. She giggled as the pup leaned into her touch, begging for her to continue. As she rubbed the pup, her breeze died down a bit and the waters stilled. Foam gently formed on the sandy shore, mixing with kelp and the occasional shell that washed up with the silt.

In the distance, the soft roar of thunder could be heard. The seal pups started and made their way towards the safety of the rocks near the shore. Freyna looked out to the sea and noticed dark clouds nearing her slowly. Graak's presence could be felt even from her location. The air around her stilled and a heaviness started to creep into the movement of the waves. Turning her head towards the cottages lining the shore, Freyna noticed mothers calling their children inside and men boarding up the windows of their homes. Heaving a sigh, Freyna made her way to the shore. Perhaps she could make her way to the village that caught her interest before the storm hit. With a light, spritely gait, she crossed the soft, sandy beach and made her way out to the village in the mountains.

As Freyna's slight form headed inland, Graak watched her miles from the shore, surrounded by the heavy winds of the impending storm, with the intensity that a father would watch over his daughter. Unlike Man, Graak and his siblings could not bear children. They would be the only ones. Being the eldest of the three, Graak took his duty of caring for his siblings with the utmost diligence. The three had no parents, for the wind does not reproduce. It is constant, never changing, always present. That is what Graak learned growing up. Normally, he loomed ever-present and ever watchful from Aerin, the northern-most tower in their majestic aerial castle. His winds commanded the obedience of both Man and nature; even his siblings. Graak's dark form stood motionless in the air miles from the shore. A darkness started to build around him, as did the heavy winds that produced the raw waves of the sea. The same waves that sink the ships of wayward travelers and privateers alike.

His eyes softened as he watched her disappear from his sight. *This is the right time. She is ready to explore the world by herself.*

*****

Freyna sat on the branch of a maple tree on the outskirts of the village of Dreth. A small smattering of cottages lay spread around, their thatched roofs and stone frames creating a picturesque scene. The flickering light of fires filled the windows. As she kicked her dangling legs, Freyna watched the families through their windows. She marveled at the children as they ran around their homes while their parents tried to catch them and put them to bed.

Despite her age, Freyna grew up sheltered and protected by her brothers, so she never experienced the world as Man did. Husbands and wives who had been married for decades sat quietly by the fire, the wives knitting and the men sharpening their tools for tomorrow's work. Other homes contained young families with children screaming and laughing as they frantically dodged out of their mothers' reach; fathers enjoying a deep belly laugh as their wives chased their children. Others housed newly-married couples sitting by the fire, holding each other and staring deeply into the soul of their partner.

Never had Freyna seen so many different familial interactions in such a short period of time. She stared intently into the windows from the safety of her tree. As the fires slowly died and darkness consumed the village, she tentatively left her perch and made her way among the cottages. Looking through the darkened windows, Freyna felt an overwhelming curiosity to explore further. Twisting slightly, she began to dance through the homes and on the rooftops. A light wind picked up around her as she let her body emulate the intrigue that she felt towards this village that captured her curiosity.

Leaping from roof to roof, she spun at the crest of her arc, creating a little howl of wind at every spin. She wanted to experience more of this village. Her soul yearned to understand these strange creatures. A bark of laughter erupted from one of the windows, causing Freyna to stop mid-spin. She dangled upside down in the air, staring at the home where the laughter rang from. Righting herself slowly, Freyna lowered herself to the ground and walked to the house at the furthest-most edge of the village. Standing on tiptoes, she pulled herself up and looked through the window. A young woman sat on a chair with a young child and dog. Confused, Freyna scanned the room for a male partner, but found none. Undaunted, she went around the side of the house and slipped in through a partially open window.

Once inside the home, she went from room to room, trying to find the woman's mate. Room by room, she left disappointed and confused. Man lived in pairs didn't they? There were plenty of them, unlike her and her brothers. Why doesn't this one follow that rule? Not so much as a picture adorned the walls or lined the mantle.

Making her way to the room with the woman, Freyna jumped up on the back of a chair and observed the woman, child and dog, invisible to their eye. The child, a boy a little under a year in age, stumbled and caught himself on the dog as he tried to walk to his mother. His shock of chestnut hair framed his face and brought out his emerald eyes. His eyelashes were long and curled gracefully, like a woman's. He looked just like his mother. As she coaxed him through his wobbly steps, she let out another bark of clear, ringing laughter. The dog, a mother herself, sat patiently as the boy grabbed her shaggy fur in his chubby little fists.

Enthralled with the interaction, Freyna watched the woman teach her child to walk for over an hour with a smile on her face. Once the boy yawned, exhausted, Freyna knew that the time to leave had come. With the grace of the wind, she slipped back out of the window and made her way home. Tomorrow she would return to the village once more. The loving interaction between mother and child differed from her experiences with her brothers. She wanted to see more of what she thought she never knew.

*****

Arriving home in the darkness, Freyna was greeted by Thuul. "How did you enjoy your time amongst Man?"

Twirling once more like the leaf that she was, Freyna replied in her airy voice, "I found one that confused me. I think I'll go back tomorrow." Without further response, she skipped off to her room, leaving Thuul smiling in the hallway. He fondly remembered his first experience with Man. Their upbeat demeanor and parental instincts captivated him as much as it did his sister. Once in her room, she slipped out of her clothes and put on a simple shift before climbing into bed where she fell asleep instantly.

II

Freyna went to visit the village every day after her chores were completed for seventeen years. As she watched the inhabitants grow, she grew to understand and care for them. At the same time, Freyna's brothers watched her develop into a young woman with the physical appearance of a sixteen-year-old. Her skin stayed pure white, her hair periwinkle hair cascaded down the middle of her back and her body became blessed with supple breasts. The children whom she watched over grew into young men and women. Some of them left the village to experience the thrill of adventure, but the majority remained home. Several new homes sprouted up over the years as new families formed within the village. One or two babies even blessed the young families over the years.

Throughout the years, she spent her time watching the young mother and her son grow into a strong family. The boy sprouted like a tree and eventually towered over his mother. His chestnut hair stayed short and the focal point of his face continued to be his eyes. His mother never seemed interested in finding a mate to help her rear her son. She didn't need one. The two of them kept a strong bond that withstood all of the silent disappointment that their neighbors directed towards them. His mother kept her spirit fierce and head held high. Nothing would break her in front of her son.

Freyna swung down from her usual perch and made her way, barefoot, through the village. About half a mile outside of the village, a clear lake nestled against the mountains. Freyna discovered the location a little over a year ago and loved to walk through the cool waters. The tranquility of the lake clearing provided a calm that stilled even Freyna's ever-shifting soul. In the empty clearing, she let out a sigh and allowed for herself to be visible to the naked eye. It was a rare treat to allow herself to be seen by the animals.

A young fawn timidly stepped into the clearing. Her nose lifted into the air and sniffed. Once she spotted Freyna, she froze, eyes wide open. Climbing slowly onto a rock, Freyna sent a small current of air towards the fawn. The fawn sniffed again as the scent of lilac flowers tickled her nose. Confused at what she saw and what she smelt, the fawn took a small step towards Freyna. Leaning her head back, Freyna held out her right hand towards the fawn and let the warmth of the sun kiss her skin.

Her body yearned to twirl and dance as she had in years prior. Oh, to be a leaf floating on the wind once more. Nothing could beat the feeling of letting oneself go and just following the ever-changing currents. Her mind pulled out of its reverie as the fawn gently started licking her hand. Freyna turned her obsidian eyes towards the fawn and met its gaze. She stared deep into the depths of the fawn and read the fawn's energy. The fawn loved to jump and run through meadows filled with wildflowers. Freyna felt a kindred spirit with this little fawn.

A sudden rustling of the bushes caused both Freyna and the fawn to start. Instantly, the fawn bolted out of the clearing and Freyna returned to her normal, invisible, state. Two young boys made their way into the clearing from the village. One boy had dark skin and a head that was completely shaven. The other was the green-eyed child whom she watched with such interest as he grew up. The two carried a line of rabbits that they caught. As they made their way further in the clearing, the dark skinned boy dropped the rabbits on the ground.

"Alaise, start the fire," the dark-skinned boy instructed.

Freyna watched as Alaise gathered up some rocks and tinder to create the fire. "Tek, how big should the fire be? Can we cook all of the rabbits on just three stones?" Tek nodded and went back to preparing the rabbits.

Freyna had never seen Tek before. *Where did he come from? He looks like one of the Easterners.* She stared at him with intrigue. Like the people of her village, Freyna also loved watching the people of the Eastern lands. They were a hardy people who, like the people in the mountains, could withstand extreme temperatures. Easterners also shared the same family ideals that the mountain people did. Unfortunately, the eastern lands usually were visited by Thuul as Graak tried to make sure that the people did not dry out from lack of rain.

Once Tek finished skinning the rabbits, Alaise went to skewer and cook them. "Wait," he commanded. "We first must give an offering to Fire in thanks of our bounty."

Alaise paused. "I'm sorry, Tek. I didn't know."

"Not a problem, friend. I'll show you how to offer proper thanks." He clapped Alaise on the back and placed the largest rabbit on the heated stones. The smell of freshly-cooking meat wafted up to Freyna's nostrils. She never saw how Man prepared food before and the sight of the skinned rabbit sizzling on the heated stone caused her to gasp. Neither Freyna nor her brothers needed to eat, so watching the young Easterner prepare the food caused her to experience a small tremor of horror. Animals should be enjoyed for their beauty, or so she thought.

Both Alaise and Tek spun around at the sound. Their eyes locked onto Freyna sitting on the rock. Her sudden shock caused her to slip into the visible spectrum. The boys each admired the simple elegance that Freyna possessed. Freyna sat glued to the stone, too afraid to return to her normal state. After a moment of quiet shock and observation, Tek dropped to a knee and Alaise followed.

"Greetings, Fair One," Tek said, bowing his head in deference to Freyna. "Your presence honors us. How may two humble men please you?"

Freyna was taken aback at his reverence. Being the youngest, she never noticed how Man offered praise and thanks to her and her brothers. She never saw the shrines that Man created in honor of them. Graak did his best to keep Thuul and Freyna grounded. "Why do you burn the rabbit if not to eat?"

"We offer thanks to Fire since he has blessed us with such a bounty. Never have we caught so many rabbits in such a short period of time." Tek faced Freyna with a measured pride that did not contain any arrogance. "We hope to stay in his good favor."

Alaise stood silently, just staring at Tek and Freyna. He seemed unable to form any words. Freyna's eyes darted from Tek to Alaise to the rabbits and back to Tek. Her eyes lingered on his. She stared deeply into the youth and watched his energies swirl within. He had strength, courage and a sincerity that not many boys his age could match. There also lay an innocence within. All of his energies flowed around in a melodious harmony that sang beautifully in her ears. Turning her gaze to Alaise, she looked into his eyes and saw pure innocence. This one shared a deep love for his mother and her struggles as she raised him by herself. He wanted only to please her and take care of her as she did him. The energies within him struck a pure, high note that resonated loudly. She smiled at what she saw. These were not boys of Fire. Fire consumed all and was unforgiving.

"Tell me," she asked, "Why do you offer thanks to Fire? You are not of Fire. You are honorable men."

Tek's jaw dropped slightly at her words. After a slight pause, Tek regained his composure and bowed his head. "Forgiveness, Fair One, but Fire also provides warmth to our bodies and gives us a way to make either food or tools. It is not something that is inherently bad."

"It may not be inherently bad to use fire," Freyna explained, "but Fire uses Man for his own gains and twists Man's thoughts. It is always best to be careful when working with Fire. He is greedy and dishonest. Whatever it takes to get what he wants, he will do. You are not like Fire, neither of you. You are caring and considerate."

Tek thought about what she said. This went against everything that he knew, but a ring of truth filled her words. Growing up he watched men who lied and cheated people for their own personal gain. Those men usually shrouded themselves with pits of fire and kept the air clouded with incense. The air often was stale and no breeze provided relief. After a few moments, Tek replied "Our offering will not go to Fire, Fair One."

"Your kind words mean so much to us," Alaise added. Alaise grew up knowing that the Wind brought refreshment and new beginnings. He did not know much about Fire. "Please, what is your name?"

Smiling brightly, she replied "Freyna". She gave a small wave and then went invisible. Once invisible, she left the boys and made her way back home.

As soon as Freyna disappeared, Tek knelt down and bowed his head in prayer. As the fats dripped onto the heated stone, Tek gave a long prayer of thanks to Freyna, whom he called Windstrider. As the prayer soared up to the heavens, Graak and Thuul paused. So fervent was Tek's prayer that the brothers smiled at whatever their little sister had done.

*****

Fire waited patiently under the stones, waiting for the burning fat to drip into his waiting grasp. As Tek began his prayer, Fire suddenly stopped as he learned that the offering was not for him. Enraged with his loss and the additional insult of having his offering go to someone else, Fire relayed his disappointment to Trap. Trap had garnered Fire's favor decades earlier and over the years became a being who lived as both Man and demi-god. Fire was generous to those who were loyal to him.

III

Trap had sandy-colored skin and fiery orange eyes. His head lay hidden under a shock of red hair. Temptation teased him as he fought the urge to set fire to a thatched cottage. The desire for destruction caused his hands to twitch with longing. His fingers began to elongate into tendrils of fire as he contemplated watching the cottage burn when suddenly he heard a whisper softly in his ear. *Go to the home of that damned Graak. His kin have wronged us.*

Hissing in frustration, Trap grabbed a bit of thatch from the roof and walked away from the home. Lighting the straw on fire, he growled into the flame, "Do it yourself! I'm busy."

Do as I say or I will come for you next.

Growling, Trap asked, "How have they wronged us?" He really did not care much for the doings of the Aetherans, but Fire did choose to bless him with the gifts of an Aetheran. Fire usually liked to find an individual every few years to bestow the gift of an elemental, an Aetheran. Wind, Earth and Water were more discerning and usually did not bless Man with such a gift. But Trap, he grew into Fire's favorite and granted him with many abilities and even extended his life. Trap at his current state rivaled some of the younger Aetherans. It would not do to lose Fire's favor.

The girl has stolen our offerings and taken them for herself. Her insolence cannot be tolerated. Go to Graak and make sure that he does not forget who he is stealing from.

A chance to exact a little retribution and sate his desire for destruction. Seemed like his day would be productive after all. "Fine, I'll take care of it." Without further word, he snuffed out the remainder of the thatch and headed further away from the home. *Graak and his kin live fairly high in the heavens. This will take a lot of energy to pull off.* Taking a deep breath, Trap looked towards the heavens and concentrated. Slowly, his body started to elongate and stretch. His body became a column of smoke as he made his way into the air.

Rising steadily, Trap caught an air current and let it propel him from current to current. Riding the currents would be the most efficient way to travel because they would take him to Graak's home without causing him to expend too much energy. Trap didn't know where they lived, but the air would take him to the right place. After several hours Trap found himself rising over a field of pristine white clouds. Above the clouds stood a glistening, crystalline castle.

Trap stayed where he was for many minutes, hovering as smoke over the clouds in order to acclimate his lungs to the lower level of oxygen. He watched the slow movement of the clouds as they circled the castle. Various shades of grey swirled past him, blending with the pureness of the layered clouds. Once he felt comfortable with the amount of oxygen that flowed through him, Trap rematerialized in his human form at the front of the castle. The clouds were surprisingly spongey and afforded him with a measured spring in his step. His soul hungered for action and, with a determined step, strode into the castle.

*****

Freyna spun slowly, shifting from foot to foot, while Thuul and Graak discussed the stifling heat that plagued the southern lands. The lands were parched and had not received any reprieve in over a year and a half. Slowly circling the room, Freyna continued to spin as Graak and Thuul debated on whether or not a week's worth of light rain or a sudden, heavy downpour would be the best way to temporarily alleviate the issue. Thuul argued that a sudden downpour would cause flash flooding, while Graak argued that a steady rain for a week could prove just as disastrous.

"Perhaps Thuul could prelude you, Graak, and prepare the earth for your mighty storms. That way you don't need to keep the storms around for so long." Freyna never stopped spinning as she offered her suggestion. If she stopped moving, the gentle breezes that cooled the earth would disappear and the air would become stale and hot. She usually only stopped for short periods of time, several hours at most when she observed her village, to prevent stale air.

Thuul thought about Freyna's idea for a moment before nodding to Graak. "She's right. This might be the best way to begin the relief."

Graak nodded in agreement. "You should bring your clouds in the late afternoon and I will follow through in the evening. If this all works correctly, we will prevent an even bigger disaster."

"Or perhaps," Trap said, "You can quit meddling in the lives of others and stay to yourselves. That way, no one loses."

The brothers spun around to face Trap, while Freyna stopped her circling and spun slower than usual. Though she continued to spin, she did not take her eyes off of the intruder.

"Our little tempest over here," Trap said, motioning to Freyna, "thought that it would be a good idea to steal obeisance from Fire and keep it for herself. Not her smartest move."

"Freyna stole nothing," Graak replied. His ever thunderous temper simmered under his calm demeanor. He would not lose his temper with this stranger. "Tell Fire that I offer my apologies, but that Freyna never sought to steal his offering."

Trap smirked. "I'm afraid that he is in no mood for apologies. He demanded payment for his stolen prayer."

"You will not be taking anything from her," Thuul snarled. "Leave now before we lose our patience with you." Winds whipped around him and the clouds around his body grew, starting to fill the room, but did not near Trap. Thuul wanted to avoid conflict if possible, but he would not back down.

"Suit yourself," Trap responded with an evil smile. Waiting for a break in Thuul's winds, Trap snapped his fingers. At the snap of his fingers, Thuul became engulfed in a ball of flame. In a panic, he dropped his winds as he screamed in pain. Freyna stopped spinning and stared in horror as her brother was destroyed by fire. Graak paused for a moment in shock once Thuul became engulfed in flames before springing into action. After the initial shock, he unleashed a fury of wind to choke out the flames. However, he was too late and the burned form of Thuul lay charred on the castle ground. Freyna cried out in dismay as she stared at her brother's remains while Graak looked on, grief-stricken.

"I'll let Fire know your position on the matter," Trap said matter-of-factly. "Enjoy your evening." In an instant, Trap became smoke once more and made his way back to earth. An Aetheran of Thuul's level could not withstand a Fire-blessed Trap. He'd spent too many years slowly wiping out the Aetheran blessed at Fire's request to let one of Thuul's skill survive.

Graak and Freyna stood rooted to the spot, unable to register what they just witnessed. Dropping to her knees, Freyna began weeping. Graak composed himself long enough to disperse his brother's ashes into the castle and meld them into the walls. Once he completed that, he walked out of the room and locked himself into his chambers.

*****

The days passed in silence. Graak did not leave his room or tend to the heavy storms. Deluges of rain pounded the westerns lands while the southern and eastern lands continued to remain starved for sustenance. Graak spent years watching Trap destroy those given gifts by the elements and could not believe that an Aetheran could succumb to such a fate. Freyna left the main hall and secluded herself in her chambers. Tears ran down her cheeks as she silently wept. Just as Graak left the storms to their own devices, Freyna no longer cared to cool the earth and let the air grow stale. Man wondered why he no longer had any gentle breezes to cool them as they went about their daily chores. Freyna did not care. She just sat and wept.

Days turned into weeks and still Freyna remained in her chambers. As the weeks passed, her skin started to slowly turn into a light shade of grey. Her hair remained a vibrant periwinkle, but her skin became the same shade as Thuul's. Freyna stopped replaying her brother's last moments in her mind and now she listened to the wind. She could hear Man's lament at the lack of breezes. One day, she heard a familiar voice discuss the lack of cooling breezes. Alaise's voice could be heard asking his mother why their normally windy village hadn't felt anything in weeks. His voice stirred something in Freyna. It had been a long time since she saw her village. She missed them and the happiness that they shared.

Night started to fall and for the first time in weeks, Freyna heard Graak leave his room and head towards Aerin. His thunderous footsteps slowly faded away and Freyna leaned her head against a wall and closed her eyes. A soft breeze ruffled her hair. Her eyes remained closed as she enjoyed a rare breeze in her room.

A sudden drop in temperature caused her eyes to open. Looking up at her ceiling, Freyna noticed a small ice crystal floating down towards her. Holding out her hands, Freyna reached up and caught it. She stared at the crystal in her hands. Unlike most, this one did not melt at her touch. She marveled at it. Looking closer at it, Freyna noticed something that caught her eye. There appeared to be two obsidian dots on the tiny ice crystal. It was a pure white, just like Freyna had been.

Staring at the tiny crystal, she nearly cried out in surprise as the two obsidian dots blinked. A gentle knocking on her door announced Graak. Freyna called for Graak to enter. Making his way down beside her, Graak looked at her hands. The tiny crystal stared up at the two of them and blinked once more. Tears of joy streamed down Graak's face and he gave a small bark of joyful laughter. It was too good to be true.

"It sure took you long enough," he exclaimed. "I almost thought that Fire succeeded in tearing apart our family." Patting Freyna on the head, he told her, "Stop crying, little one. Everything will be alright. The circle has been completed once more." Graak then exited the room and returned to Aerin.

Freyna watched her brother leave with a look of confusion on her face. Looking down at her hands, she realized that the crystal looked very familiar. Tears of joy rolled down her cheeks. Fire tried to break apart their family through revenge and he almost succeeded. However, no matter what he tried, it didn't matter; the wind doesn't die.

What Makes a Man

Written by

T. M. Lowe

Officer Jessie Parker's life nearly ended 3.8 seconds ago. She and her partner were scheduled for what should have been light duty that night: parking their marked cruiser in a high-traffic area of the seedier side of Florenceville to serve as a warning and general crime deterrent. In most cases, simply showing an active police presence was enough to keep troublemakers at bay. So, Officer Daniel Jones had selected a good spot to camp out, parked the car, and the two proceeded to keep an eye on the intersection while they chatted.

"During that chase last week," Daniel said, glancing at Jessie briefly from the corner of his eye, "what exactly did you mean by 'sandwich'?"

"Oh, the whole 'I could use a good sandwich right about now' thing?" she asked, then laughed and started to explain. "You know, we were on one side of the perps, Pittman was coming from the other side." She demonstrated the maneuver with her hands. "Like two pieces of bread coming together against meat and cheese to form a sandwich?"

"The four-door sedan containing three robbery suspects was... meat and cheese?"

"Jokes lose their punch when you have to explain them." She sighed. "Don't worry about it. The guys find my humor dubious at best, so you're not alone."

He made a non-committal humming sound. Then, he cracked a small smirk.

Jessie narrowed her green eyes at him. "Unless you actually *did* get the joke," she said, "and you're just screwing around with me."

"I can neither confirm nor deny."

"Greeeeeat," she drawled out, tossing her hands in the air. "Put a bunch of artificially intelligent robots in a police station with the hopes and intent of them learning the more ambiguous and non-linear parts of human decision-making and what do they pick up on the best? Dry, deadpan humor." She grinned and raised an eyebrow at him. "You, sir, are a hot mess."

"Your assessment is inaccurate," replied Daniel. "I am not 'hot'. My temperature levels remain steady." Then, in a lowered voice, he added, "I am a well-oiled machine." He turned his head towards her just long enough to waggle his eyebrows before resuming his watch on the intersection.

"Oh, my God," Jessie groaned as she buried her face in her hands and laughed. When she recovered, her face was red. "Who? *Who* taught you that? Was it Biggs?" she asked, shaking her head and trying to suppress another peal of chuckles. "It had to be Biggs. *Of course* the main thing he'd want to impart on you guys is how to awkwardly flirt."

Daniel suddenly cocked his head like a dog hearing a sound outside of human hearing range before quickly moving to cover her body with his. The cruiser's windows shattered and the sound of gunfire assaulting metal filled the air. The urge to try and return fire was strong, but Daniel kept Jessie pinned down.

Then, almost as soon as it had begun, the shooting stopped. Daniel let her go, grimacing, and turned to catch a glimpse of the fleeing vehicle. From that angle, it was easy for Jessie to see the hole in his uniform and the steady stream of orange fluid seeping out. She scrambled for the two-way radio. "This is Unit 462. We just had a drive-by on our cruiser. Officer injured."

"We should pursue them," Daniel said.

"Like hell we should!" she blustered. "You've got a bullet rattling around in you."

The android rolled his wounded shoulder and winced, narrowing his blue eyes and grunting. "No," he corrected, "it is securely lodged in the structural frame of my shoulder plate."

"Oh, lovely," she scoffed, "because that's *much* more comforting."

A man's gruff voice crackled over the radio, "Who's shot? Location?" Before she could answer, the voice cut in again, irritated. "Oh, it's you, Parker. I'm guessing you mean AO-23?"

"Yes," she answered through gritted teeth. "*Officer Daniel* was shot."

"How bad? Is the unit down?"

"Negative," said Daniel. "Bullet lodged in right shoulder, but non-lethal. Fluid loss minimal so far. Performance currently unhindered." He put the car into gear, activated the lights and siren, and began driving in the direction their attackers had fled.

Jessie glared at him. Then, she keyed the radio again. "We are currently in pursuit and could use some back-up. Blue SUV heading southbound on Jay Avenue, about two blocks from Murray Theatre."

Buildings rushed past her window as Daniel increased their speed.

"License number 5KS G4W," he added.

"Parker, this is Biggs in Unit 328," came the man's voice over the radio. "We're en route from Tavary Square, ETA 15."

"Make that a double from Pittman in Unit 759, but from Southside," said another. "Sandwich time again so soon?"

Jessie heard them both snicker before cutting off their radio transmissions.

However, the momentary humor died when she saw a man with a pistol hang out of the passenger window of the SUV as they caught up to it. Daniel saw it as well and gunned the gas pedal, ramming the front end of their cruiser into the back bumper of the fleeing vehicle. The gunman quickly retreated back inside the SUV as it swerved to the right and dove down a narrow side street. Daniel pulled the steering wheel and forced the cruiser to make the hard turn in pursuit, tires chirping with agitation.

Jessie cursed, grabbing the door armrest to steady herself as the car slung through the turn and sped up again. If she were a little better aim while in motion or if she were driving instead of Daniel, the chase would end very quickly with a few well-placed bullets into the rear tires. As it stood, she was afraid of the risk of collateral damage if she tried firing at the SUV, which would encourage them to fire back as well, and a high-speed chase was already dangerous to any early-bird pedestrians. Daniel's computer brain with its advanced targeting systems would have some challenge, but not too much, in hitting the SUV's tires – but he couldn't be expected to try and do that while also controlling the cruiser.

And while injured, Jessie reminded herself. She looked at her partner's shoulder injury again and frowned. The orange, synthetic blood appeared to be leaking out faster as the dark stain on his uniform grew. She figured it was due to the increased stress of their situation, as well as all the maneuvering Daniel had to do as they zig-zagged through the streets.

She was no expert on the android units, but she'd learned enough about them to know that they responded to situations in a very similar fashion to humans. Just as a person experienced the rush of adrenaline, so did the androids, whose systems would speed up to help them move and calculate faster. As a result, their internal mechanisms heated up, but were kept at reasonable temperatures by their fluid and coolant flow.

Unless, of course, that unit had a bullet hole that ripped open some tubing and led to those fluids spilling instead. It wasn't so much a risk of bleeding out like a human would, but rather of frying internal circuitry. Some of that could be replaced, but not all of it. Organ failure was a very bad prospect no matter if you were biological or mechanical. Daniel was operating on a countdown clock and there wasn't much Jessie could do about it.

Frustrated, she dug around underneath her seat for the first aid kit. There wasn't one for androids, but perhaps there'd be something of use. Anything to give her something to do to try and help, aside from keeping

Biggs and Pittman updated over the radio and watching the world rush by. She pulled out a gauze pad and figured it was worth a try.

"What are you doing?" Daniel asked as Jessie firmly pressed the bandage against the hole in his shoulder.

"Trying to help you keep fluids in."

"While I appreciate the gesture," he said, "that unfortunately will not work. It does not clot like your blood. Until the tubes are clamped and repaired, it will flow."

She closed her eyes and sighed. "Is there *anything* I can do?"

"Just keep guiding the others to us," he replied. "We need to end this soon."

There were many people, a few of them fellow officers down at the station, who said that androids were incapable of actual, real feelings. They could mimic them, but that didn't mean they actually understood them or felt them. They weren't people. They weren't "real". They were made, not born, and therefore lesser than human, lesser even than animals, who were proven capable of some level of emotion.

Jessie was not one of those people. Her beliefs were further cemented when she saw the pinched look on Daniel's face, the way his human-like, synthetic skin pulled and wrinkled in all the right places. He looked worried, perhaps even fearful, and that was not exactly an emotion she thought he'd mindlessly mimic like a mockingbird for her sake. It would serve no purpose.

Biggs and Pittman were not far away now, and they both had android officer partners with them. Jessie took some comfort from that, knowing that her own partner was not likely to be up for a prolonged scene once they got the SUV stopped. The chase had led them out of the city proper and into the outskirts. While that meant less cover, that also meant fewer civilians. It would just be them and the gunmen.

"Okay, guys," Pittman chimed in on the radio, "I've got the spike strip set up about 200 feet past the railroad tracks. How're we lookin'?"

Jessie replied, "We're almost there. I can see the tracks up ahead."

That was around the time she also saw the railroad crossing lights begin to flash. She quickly looked left, right, and then spotted the freight train further down on their right, approaching at a fast rate. It was highly questionable if the SUV would make the crossing in time to beat the train, and even more questionable if their cruiser pursuing the SUV would.

She glanced at Daniel. He was blinking rather rapidly, a distant look in his eyes. "You okay, Daniel?" she asked hesitantly. When there was no response, she grew a little louder. "Danny?"

"Calculating."

Jessie looked at the SUV again and saw they had sped up. Apparently, the gunmen were going to try and beat the train. She felt their cruiser pick up speed to match. "Danny, what are your calculations saying about this?"

"Still calculating."

"I think this is a poor decision," she warned.

"There is an 80.6 percent chance the train will not be at the crossing at the same time we are at our current speed," Daniel answered, pushing down further on the gas pedal.

The approaching freighter let out a long, loud warning blast from its horn as it neared the intersection.

Jessie turned and pinned him with frightened eyes. "Daniel, listen to yourself," she pleaded. "That's also saying there's a twenty percent chance we get wiped into paste by that train. Is it worth the risk?"

The train horn screamed out again, this time for an extended length of time, followed by the screech of locomotive brakes desperately engaging to try and slow the engine down. The android's arms began to quiver and his cheeks flinched as if he were grinding his jaws.

"You're not operating at peak capacity," Jessie pushed. "Can you truly trust your calculations right now? Enough to risk both our lives with them?"

Daniel's eyes closed for a moment. When he opened them again, the cruiser lurched with sudden braking. Tires squealed in protest. The SUV ahead of them charged through the railroad crossing arms, sending splintered wood flying. The cruiser stopped inches from the tracks just before the freight train roared by, horn still bleating and brakes still trying to slow the unyielding beast. Jessie stared wide-eyed at the blur of cars rushing by, then fell back against her seat and closed her eyes, letting out the breath she'd been holding. When she opened them again, her partner was slumped over the steering wheel.

"Daniel?" she asked, voice wavering.

Weakly, he answered, "I do not feel well."

Jessie grabbed the in-car radio. "Biggs, Pittman," she called. "Sorry, but we got caught by the train. Perps made it through. Danny's fading fast, so I'm taking us back to the barn."

"No worries, Jessie, we got this," Biggs replied. "See you back there soon. Danny, take care, brother."

After helping her partner to the passenger side of their cruiser, Jessie was grateful that the drive back to their station was quick, quiet, and uneventful. With Daniel leaning heavily against her right side, she opened the door and was even more grateful to see Gerald Thompson waiting for them. He swooped in on the other side to gently support Daniel and the three made their way back to The Pen, a barracks area they used to house their android officers when not out on patrol.

"Awful early for you to be here, Gerald," Jessie commented. "Although I couldn't be happier to see you right now, that's for sure."

A bashful grin crept across his face. "Yeah, Squirrels gave me a call when he heard how things went down over the radio," Gerald explained. "Didn't figure the night shift guy was ready to fly solo on a tech operation a little more complicated than figuring out why someone's laptop is being grumpy. Heh."

A few of the off-duty android officers gave the trio inquisitive looks as they passed through the first room of The Pen, then they went back to their previous activities. Once through the small hallway that served as the androids' locker room, they found Roger Tassing waiting for them in the maintenance room. He had been proactive and grabbed everything that looked like it could possibly be used in android repair and laid it out across the workbench.

"Taz, the main things we're gonna need are clamps and size C-6 tubing," Gerald said as they led Daniel into a sitting position on a waist-height table in the middle of the room.

"Already got it," he answered. "I already got... uh... *everything*. I think."

"Good, good," said Gerald. He wiped a rag over his face and repositioned the overhead light. "Come around here, Taz, and give me a hand."

"How can I help?" Jessie asked.

"First, we gotta get his shirt off," answered Gerald, "and then if you can just help keep him relatively still for us?"

Jessie nodded and did as she was told. Daniel grimaced and grunted as they maneuvered his arms out of the ruined uniform and let it fall to the floor. Then, she pulled a chair up in front of the android so that she was facing him. "Hey," she said to him softly, "look at me, buddy. Gonna need you to stay as still as possible, okay?"

"I heard."

Her partner had never been hurt this badly before, so this was a new experience for both of them. She didn't know if it would be as simple as switching out some parts and then sewing him back up or something more complex. She knew that their synthetic skin could close back up on its own relatively quickly for minor injuries, but this wasn't exactly minor.

When Gerald started digging into the shoulder to assess the extent of the damage, the android flinched and moaned.

"Gonna need him more still than that!"

The look Daniel gave her broke Jessie's heart. He was trying so hard to follow directions, but it was clear that he was in pain.

"Can't he just lay face-down on the table while you do this?" she asked.

"Harder angle to work at," Gerald replied. "Need him sitting up."

Jessie let off a frustrated sigh. "Can you at least give him something for the pain?"

Gerald stopped and gave her a look that asked if she was serious. When he realized she was, his features softened into sympathy. "Sadly, androids need to know when their bodies are taking damage so that they can stop doing whatever is damaging it. Like us," he explained. "And, sadly, that does appear to equate into pain for them. Like us. Although, they do have a much higher tolerance threshold than we do." He scowled. "And unlike us, the powers that be view them as sophisticated machines. Big walking, talking computers, nothing more. There are no painkillers for machines. They don't exist. At all."

Jessie frowned.

Gerald continued, "And before you ask, no, there is no off switch for either the pain sensors or his consciousness. While he appears to sleep when he's in a recharge cycle, he can't get into that state while his body is registering damage. A really awesome catch twenty-two." He sighed. "Trust me, Jessie, I've tried to think of everything. But until the people in charge of stuff and the people that have money to invest in stuff start seeing android officers as more than just an expensive computer experiment or really fancy tools for you guys to ride around with and take bullets for you, nothing's going to change."

Jessie didn't know what to say to that, so she hung her head. In all honesty, there was nothing *to* say. Taking a deep breath, she nodded. Then, she looked back up and grasped Daniel's hands, giving them a light, gentle squeeze. Her eyes caught his and she smiled at him. "Whenever it starts to hurt too much," she said, "just squeeze my hands. It'll help."

The android gave her a dubious look. "But I could hurt you," he countered. "I have strong hands."

"Well, then, you'll simply have to focus on not crushing them, won't you?" Jessie replied, giving him a confident grin. "Remember your training on using non-lethal force to subdue a suspect?"

He nodded.

"There might come a time when you'll have to do that after you've been injured," she continued. "So, this can be practice, yeah?"

"Yes, ma'am," he answered quietly, eyes glancing down, unsure.

"Hey," she said, giving his hands a small tug, "look at me." When he did, she continued, "You don't have to 'ma'am' me. I'm not your superior. You're my partner, Danny." She squeezed his hands again. "You're my *friend*. Okay?"

He glanced away again and cleared his throat, looking for all the world as if he were a bit embarrassed. Jessie smirked. She suspected that if he'd actually had blood vessels, Daniel might have been blushing. He looked back at her sheepishly, then smiled. He gave her hands a squeeze back. "Okay," he said, "I am ready."

It was an incredibly uncomfortable experience for them both, but the two partners got through it as they did any other situation when on patrol – together as a team. Whenever Daniel started to tense up too much, Jessie would ground him again with soft words and encourage him to squeeze her hands, giving him something to focus on besides what his pain receptors were unhelpfully telling him.

Gerald was mercifully quick. Once he removed the bullet and replaced the ruptured tubing and other assorted bits, he sutured the hole and gave

Daniel a light pat on the left shoulder. "All done, buddy," he said. "You did good." As Jessie helped the android off the operating table, Gerald handed him a bottle of orange liquid. "Make sure you drink the whole thing before you settle in to recharge," he explained, "and in about 24 hours, you'll be good as new."

"Thank you," Daniel said.

"Um, yeah," replied Gerald, scratching at the back of his neck self-consciously. "No problem, Daniel."

Jessie nodded her thanks as well and walked with the android out to the main area of The Pen. She did a double-take when she saw Biggs sitting on the couch playing with his phone. Catching their movement from his peripheral vision, the bearded man stood up and turned to them, looking Daniel up and down.

"How you holdin' up, Danny boy?" he asked.

"I have been better," replied the android.

"That bullet would've been in me if it hadn't been for him," Jessie added.

Biggs looked impressed and nodded his head. "Nice goin', dude!"

"Thanks," Daniel replied. Glancing at one of the empty bunks, he added, "It has been a rather long day, so…"

"Say no more, my man," Biggs replied, taking the hint. "Just wanted to make sure y'all made it back in one piece. Or mostly one piece, at least." The large, bear of a man chuckled. He turned to Jessie and signaled for her to walk with him out of The Pen. She gave Daniel a parting wave, then followed Biggs.

"Wanted you to know we hauled your perps in," he added. "Already got 'em booked and sleeping arrangements. My report's in already. Cap'n says that's enough for now and you can fill yours out tomorrow."

"Thanks," said Jessie, "and, actually, I think I'll go see Tinnerman myself before I go."

"Woof," Biggs replied, shaking his head. "Well, good luck with that. As for me, I'm gonna go home and crash. Which is exactly what *you* should be doing. Like, right now. Rather than seein' the Cap."

"Good night, Biggs," she said and waved him off as she picked up her pace towards Captain Tinnerman's office. Now that the shock and adrenaline of their shift was wearing off, an old anger of hers was resurfacing. It was an issue she'd brought up before, back when they first instituted the AO program at their station, but it had always been a hypothetical – though very possible – situation. Now that it had actually happened, she hoped it might lead to a different result when she brought it up again.

The captain's office door was open, so Jessie strode in and shut the door behind her. Loudly. That grabbed Captain Tinnerman's attention from his newspaper and coffee. "Ah, Officer Parker, good morning!" he greeted, setting the newspaper down.

"A word, sir?" she asked sharply.

"Yes, of course!" he replied, then gestured to the chair across from his desk. "Have a seat." Jessie approached his desk, but remained standing. "Biggs and Pittman already filed their reports," he continued, "so you can wait and submit yours after a good sleep, if you'd like. I heard you had a rather eventful shift last night."

"Eventful is certainly a word for it, sir," she said, her voice clipped and staccato as she struggled to control her anger. "One that ended with me having to try and keep my partner focused off of his pain while Gerald dug a bullet out of his shoulder. A bullet that otherwise would have hit me if it hadn't been for his selfless actions last night."

"That's excellent," stated the captain. "He protected you. That's what they're supposed to do. And Gerald was able to treat him, like he's supposed to do."

"Yeah. Care to know where he took the bullet?" she asked. When there was no response but anticipatory silence, she continued, "In the back of his right shoulder."

Captain Tinnerman shifted a little uncomfortably, but otherwise maintained eye contact with her.

"And I presume we all know what protects a right shoulder from a bullet?"

"There's no need to take a smart tone with me, Parker," he barked. "Yes, I know, a bulletproof vest would have prevented–"

"Would have prevented an hour of whimpering in agony!" she yelled. "These are *not* just machines. These are creatures we have created that feel pain. They have no choice in the matter. We made them and put them here."

"You don't think I recognize that?" he shouted back.

"No, I don't," she answered. "We treat our *dogs* better than we do them. At least all our canine units have proper protection–"

"I can't get the funding right now," Captain Tinnerman retorted, his tone defensive. "I tried, Jessie, I really did. I've already told you that."

"Jesus Christ, we have funding for *virus protection* on our *desktops!*" she cried out. "*They're* better protected than the very android officers who are out there every day risking their lives with us!"

"The mayor's office refused to increase our budget."

"I'd be more than happy to take Daniel's bloodied uniform to the mayor's office and drop it on his desk myself."

"That will *not* be happening," he ordered. "I've told you before that if you feel this damn strongly about it, put your money where your mouth is."

"You sign my paychecks, *sir*," Jessie fumed, "so you know damn well I can't afford to freelance buy vests for all our AO units and Daniel refuses to wear one if the others can't be equally protected. An awfully thoughtful and noble notion for a mere *machine*."

Captain Tinnerman pinched the bridge of his nose and closed his eyes. Despite the cup of coffee, he suddenly looked utterly exhausted. "Jessie," he said softly, "I don't know what else you expect me to do here. I understand. I sympathize. I actually *do* care about them. I know you think I don't, but I do. You're *all* my officers – human, canine, and otherwise – but there are only so many things in my control. Getting our budget upped enough to cover this expense simply isn't one of those things. Not right now. I really am sorry."

"Then you're not trying hard enough–"

"Officer Parker," he interrupted in a terse tone filled with finality. "It's been a long night and a tough shift. You're tired. Go home and rest. Preferably before you say something you'll come to regret."

Jessie's mouth opened and closed twice as she fought with herself about getting a last word in edgewise. However, she recognized when a conversation was finished. She bid her superior officer a good night, turned tail, and stormed out.

*****

"Fancy seeing you here," Jessie said with a hint of humor in her voice.

Gerald turned and shot her a raised eyebrow from behind his black-rimmed glasses. "I could say the same about you. I didn't think you were scheduled for a shift today." When he took in the sight of her jeans and T-shirt, he quickly amended himself. "And clearly you *aren't* scheduled for a shift today, so to what do we owe this pleasure?"

He emphasized the plural form by sweeping his arm out to indicate all the AO units hanging around The Pen. Michael, Edward, and Theodore were laid out on cots recharging; Franklin was interfacing with a desktop computer in the corner; and Nicholas sat on the couch with Gerald in front of a television screen and gaming console.

Daniel was parked in front of the other desktop computer, but spun around at the sound of his partner's voice. He gave her a smile and she answered with a quick wink.

"I was on my way to my parents' and figured I'd stop in and see how everyone was doing," she replied, shifting her attention back to Gerald. "You know, wellness check on the poor schmucks spending the holiday alone at the office."

"It's not so bad," he said with a shrug. "Better than spending it alone."

"Gerald, you know you're always welcome to come hang with my family," she said. "I've told you before they're cool. Generally no fights, no politics; just companionship, good food, and drinking. The worst that could happen is my aunt and uncle beating you at corn toss and then rubbing your face in it the rest of the night."

Gerald laughed. "Nah," he answered. "I appreciate it. I really do. But I'm not a people person, you know that. Plus, I gotta be here in case any of them gets called out today and comes back hurt. I'd rather keep these guys company anyway." He smiled at the android next to him. "Besides, I'm about to finally beat Nickster here at *Dogs of War 5* in a death match!"

"How?" she asked incredulously. "How on earth are you beating an android at a twitch shooter? That's like beating someone who's hacked the game."

"I made it more sporting for him," Nicholas explained, "by reducing my hand-eye reaction time by 43.6 percent."

Jessie raised an eyebrow. "You can do that?"

"Yes."

"Check it out," said Gerald. He picked up a foam stress ball from the end table and turned to the android. "Nickster, think fast!" Nicholas turned quickly enough. Then, Gerald tossed the ball at his head. It bounced off harmlessly and rolled across the floor. Seconds later, the officer reached up towards his forehead as if to catch the ball in mid-flight.

"It's like shooting fish in a barrel," she admonished, shaking her head. "Why? How is that fun?"

"It *is* Christmas, after all," Nicholas replied. "As Gerald said, it is the season of giving."

Gerald looked offended. "Hey!"

Jessie doubled over in laughter. "Oh, wow," she said, "Did he just throw shade by implying he's giving you a win? Because I think that's what just happened."

"Yeah, yeah," grumbled Gerald. "Aren't your parents gonna wonder where you are soon? Skedaddle, missy!"

"Before I deliver my Christmas goodies?" she bantered back. "Really, now? You know you want my goodies."

"Wait, what?" he asked, tune changing.

Jessie smirked, then shed the backpack from her shoulders and rooted around in it. After a moment of digging, she tossed a bag of home-made cookies to Gerald. "Merry Christmas, you doofus."

His face lit up. "Awww, Jess!"

"Now, where are the boys' rations for the evening?"

The tech keeper already had a cookie shoved in his mouth, so he pointed towards a specific locker against the back wall. Jessie closed the distance, opened the door, and pulled out six rectangular, wrapped bars. She tucked one safely away into a side pocket on her backpack, then opened the other five and dumped them into a large plastic bag of powdered sugar. She shook it around a bit to get all the bars coated in the sweet substance before placing the whole bag into the locker and closing the door.

At Gerald's questioning look, she said, "A little extra holiday flavor for them."

"How thoughtful," he drawled. "I'll try to remember the intent behind it when I'm helping them clear out blocked tubing later."

"Drama queen," she teased, briefly sticking her tongue out at him. Then, turning a little more serious, she added, "Although, I do admit I came here with an ulterior motive." Jessie glanced over at Daniel, who was watching her every move. "I was hoping my partner might like to join me. Get out of The Pen for a bit. Be exposed to some new people who aren't just his fellow officers or criminals."

Gerald squirmed. While the human officers had been encouraged to take their android partners out as often as possible, doing so off-hours was not exactly encouraged. It was not technically forbidden, per se, but also not really a thing anyone had tried to explore yet. There were liability issues, after all. What the androids did while on duty was considered part of their training. Outside of that safety net? Not so much.

"It's Christmas, Gerald," she said. "It's a family gathering at someone's private residence. It can't be that big of a deal."

"Promise you'll bring him back right after?"

"I promise."

"Promise no weirdness is gonna happen?"

"Oh, now, this *is* my family we're talking about," Jessie joked. "You know that I cannot, in good conscience, make that kind of promise. There will be weirdness. There's always weirdness."

He sighed and rubbed a hand over his face. "Can you at least promise the weirdness won't permanently affect him in any way?"

She thought for a moment, rubbing her chin, and waited. And waited. And waited some more until the silence became unbearable. Finally, she responded, "Yeah, I can probably commit to that much, at least."

Gerald sighed again, rolled his eyes in extra dramatic fashion for Jessie's amusement, and shooed the two of them out as quickly as possible so he could resume his game with Nicholas.

It didn't take long for them to arrive at Jessie's parents' house and, once they did, the number of vehicles parked all over the place told them they were fashionably late. Daniel offered to help carry in the presents while Jessie grabbed the tray of cookies for the food table. Shortly after, the two were enveloped in a sea of greetings, hugs, cheek kisses, and general good feelings. Once the offerings were dropped off at the appropriate places inside, Jessie led Daniel out into the backyard where the majority of her relatives were gathered.

The pair was noticed in short order and Jessie officially introduced Daniel to everyone. As she had predicted, he was immediately accepted at face value before most everyone returned to their prior activities. Daniel was scooped up by her brother, Christopher, and her nephew, Todd, while she found herself led aside by her mother, Nancy.

"So," Nancy started, "you finally bring a man with you to meet the family and he turns out to not actually be a man?" She chuckled softly as if trying to keep the tone light.

Jessie felt nothing but judgment. "Really, Mom?" she responded. "No, 'Hi, how've you been?' or 'How's the job going, sweetie?' Instead, we jump straight into my love life status and the biological versus non-biological merits of my coworker?"

"It was a joke, dear, don't fly off the handlebars," Nancy said flatly. "I'd have said the same thing if you'd brought one of those police dogs with you instead."

Sighing, Jessie closed her eyes and pinched the bridge of her nose. "Sorry," she said, "but you wouldn't believe the battle it is to get anyone to view them with respect."

Her mother was silent for a moment. Then, with a hint of trepidation in her voice, she asked, "Do they actually need respect?" At Jessie's angry look, she added, "As in, do they feel disrespected somehow?"

"Well, no, I don't think Daniel's ever mentioned feeling disrespected, but–"

"The paper says they're tools," Nancy interrupted. "They're there to help keep our human officers safe, to keep *you* safe. That's what they were made for, that's their purpose, right?"

"Yes, but by that definition, you could call our dogs tools, too."

"Dogs are born, not made."

"I beg to differ," Jessie argued. "Dogs have been created from thousands of years of careful breeding so that specific traits exist. That didn't come naturally. They were made. Created."

"But they're still *born*," countered her mother. "Living creatures simply take a higher precedence than man-made objects."

"Daniel is more than just an object. He can think–"

"Computers can think." Nancy interrupted. "They are still objects."

"He can learn."

"My phone can learn," her mother countered. "It learned to recognize my accent and now talk-to-text works almost seamlessly. It's still an object."

"He can feel, *mother*," Jessie growled.

"How do you know this?" Nancy asked. "You already said he can think and learn. Mimicking facial expressions and body language doesn't mean actually feeling them. A parrot repeating phrases it's heard doesn't mean it knows the definitions of the words or the subtle context contained within them."

"Is there some particular reason we're spending Christmas arguing?" Jessie asked heatedly.

"I worry about you, Jessie," she confessed. "The way you talk about it on the phone sometimes. It's like you're anthropomorphizing your car. Be careful where you put your feelings."

"At least I *have* feelings," she spat.

"Yo, Jessie!" her brother yelled from across the yard. "We could use you over here!"

"Duty calls," she said sarcastically, turning and leaving before Nancy could continue the argument.

At the far end of the yard, Christopher stood beside Daniel and Todd. The young boy had a remote control in his hands. On the ground between the three was a small metal aircraft that vaguely resembled a helicopter, but had fixed wings topped with propellers on either side of the fuselage. It buzzed like an angry bumblebee, lifted off the ground by a few inches, and then promptly fell over sideways in the grass. Her nephew growled in frustration.

Jessie gave Christopher a grateful look. "Oh, my God," she sighed, "thank you!"

He chuckled and ran a hand through his dirty blonde hair out of nervous habit. "Don't mention it," he replied. "I know how Mom can be and you clearly looked like you needed rescuing." At his sister's pinched look, he quickly changed the subject. "So, we actually did need you over here." He pointed to the toy. "What would you call that?"

She gave him a slightly dumbfounded look. "Um, okay, that's kind of a weird question," she said, then glanced down at the object again. "I dunno, a helicopter?"

He grunted. "Is there anything else you'd call it? Any sort of different name?"

"Uh." She raised an eyebrow at him in confusion. "A remote-controlled aircraft?"

"Or...?" he asked again, lightly nodding his head towards a box on the nearby table.

Jessie glanced at the lettering and sighed. "I'm guessing the correct answer is a drone?"

"There, see!" Christopher shouted triumphantly, giving Daniel a pointed look.

Daniel furrowed his brows. "You influenced her answer by leading her to the inaccurate box labeling," he accused. "That does not count as an unbiased opinion."

"Okay, what's going on here?" she asked. "Because if you pulled me out of one argument just to throw me into another one, I'm gonna have to bust some skulls."

"Not really an argument, per se," her brother said, holding his hands up defensively, "rather a disagreement. Poindexter here," he nodded towards her partner, "said this isn't actually a drone."

"Because it is not," interjected Daniel. "It is technically a UAV - an unmanned aerial vehicle guided by a human remotely."

"But the box says it's a drone," Christopher countered, "and everyone else calls it a drone."

"A drone is also a UAV, but those generally carry ordinance," Daniel argued, "and they can navigate autonomously or on a pre-set flight path."

"Um, guys?" Jessie said.

"Does it really matter, though?" Christopher asked. "They both basically mean the same thing."

"Guys?"

"They do not mean the same thing," Daniel answered. "That would be like saying artificial intelligence and virtual intelligence are the same because both are computer programming."

"DINGBATS!" Jessie shouted. When they both looked at her, she pointed up.

In one of the mid-level branches of an oak tree, the toy helicopter spun and whirled its propellers in vain. It had launched into a thick nest of leaves and managed to imbed sticks between its rotor blades, effectively trapping it. Down below, Todd bit his lower lip with tears in his eyes, desperately working the controller in his hands to try and free his new toy. It didn't budge.

"Here, let me try," Christopher said softly, taking the remote from his son. After several minutes of working the joysticks every which way he could, the chopper was no less stuck. Todd started to cry.

"What if we got a ladder?" suggested Jessie. "We could prop it up against the trunk enough for me to reach the lowest branch and climb up from there."

"No way," said Nancy as she walked up. "You'll break your neck. Look at the branch it's on, it's too small to support much weight."

"Maybe we could hit it with something and knock it loose?"

Christopher was apparently one step ahead of her thought process, picking up a football from the assorted mess of kids toys in the yard. He threw it with all his force, hitting a branch a few feet below the one with the trapped helicopter. When he picked the ball back up to try again, Daniel motioned for it. He tossed it to the android. Daniel looked up at the offending branch, drew back, and hurled the football. It made a direct hit on the correct limb, mere inches from hitting the helicopter itself, but the effort still failed to free it. Actually hitting the chopper itself could possibly free it, but was more likely to damage it.

"Everyone stand back," warned Harold, Christopher and Jessie's father. He'd brought out a fishing pole from the garage. With a quick flick, he hooked the branch and started pulling back on the rod, shaking the limb aggressively. After several heated moments of battle, the line broke and the chopper remained stubbornly stuck. Harold's shoulders drooped in defeat.

"This is the worst Christmas ever!" Todd yelled. He flopped to the ground with the sort of unabashed drama only a ten-year-old could muster and started loudly sobbing.

Everyone looked at each other helplessly, the mood dampened. Daniel, meanwhile, looked thoughtfully between the child, the tree branch, and the ladder propped against the side of the shed.

"Come on, buddy," Christopher said, patting Todd's back and trying to console him. "We'll buy you a new one when the stores open tomorrow."

"But Santa brought it!" the boy wept. "That one's special!"

"Daniel, what are you doing?" Jessie asked when she spotted her partner placing the ladder against the tree.

"I can reach it," he explained. "I calculated."

"No!" she said emphatically. "Mom's right, that branch looks too small to support weight."

"I am made of lighter materials than you."

"Danny, *no*," she insisted. "Setting aside the fact that I really don't want you getting hurt, if you fall and get damaged, we are *both* in deep trouble with Captain Tinnerman."

"Then I will not fall," he answered matter-of-factly.

"Officer Daniel Jones," Jessie said in her sternest voice, crossing her arms and fixing him with a stare.

The android turned from the ladder to look at her fully. Whereas his body had been more relaxed before, he now stood up straight at attention with shoulders rolled back, hands balled into fists along the outside leg seams of his dark blue off-duty jumpsuit.

"Is that a direct order, ma'am?" he asked in a very even and emotionless tone.

Jessie cursed internally. When the androids were first produced, they were military models. They all looked the same and functioned on VI programming, meaning all they could do was follow a set path of directions and logic. They could not think for themselves and had no capacity to learn or evolve and, honestly, she suspected the military liked it that way. The perfect soldier that never questioned orders, never showed physical pain or emotional remorse, never slowed down, and was perfectly expendable in the eyes of everybody else.

When a private security corporation wanted to extend and test the use of androids on the home front, they adapted the military model and completely overhauled it for testing in the police force. Unique facial casts were made to help avoid the "uncanny valley" feeling for the human officers who would be training and working alongside them. Artificial intelligence replaced virtual intelligence so they could learn and process fast-developing situations to form logical orders of their own to follow. In essence, their androids went from the equivalent of assembly line automatons to full-blown individual recruits on par with any student in police academy.

However, being machines, they still had a built-in safety switch. For all the free will the android officers were allowed, they could not disobey anything that was issued as a direct order. But, much like trying to discipline a rebellious teenager, giving a direct order generally had the negative effect of eroding the relationship, going from mentor-student to superior-subordinate. Most human officers tried to avoid such situations whenever possible, unless absolutely necessary to override a life-or-death situation.

Jessie had never once issued a direct order to Daniel, and she didn't intend to start now. "No," she finally said, sighing heavily with acceptance. "No, it's not. Do what you think is best. I'll trust your judgment."

The android smiled at her, stance relaxing. Then, he turned and started up the ladder. Once at the top step, he stretched out, got a firm grasp on the lowest branch of the tree, and carefully hauled himself up. A hush fell over the gathered party as everyone watched him pick his way up the old oak tree. Even Todd, still sniffling and rubbing at his red eyes, sat up and joined the adults in wide-eyed observation.

When Daniel reached the troublesome limb, he wrapped his legs around it and slowly inched out towards the entrapped helicopter. He paused every few moments and held perfectly still whenever the branch groaned and dipped in a way he didn't like. Finally, he arrived at the spot. Bracing himself with his right arm, he reached out with his left hand and pulled the red chopper free of its confines.

"Would someone kindly fly it down?" he called out. "I fear dropping it might break it."

As the officer held the helicopter out in the palm of his hand, Christopher grabbed the remote and floated the toy down to Todd. The boy jumped up excitedly, grabbing the chopper and hugging it to his chest. Then, he turned and watched as Daniel carefully descended the tree.

Jessie didn't breathe until her partner's feet safely hit the ground.

Her family broke out in a small round of applause. Daniel looked around at them with a lop-sided grin and brows drawn together, an expression that she recognized as his way of blushing – she'd noted that he only ever did it when receiving praise. Her father walked up and clapped a hand against the android's shoulder. When he did so, Daniel grabbed something off of his belt loop and handed it to Harold. The old man laughed and showed everyone that it was the fish hook he'd lost up in the tree when the line broke. At the same time, her nephew ran up and latched onto her partner's leg in a death-grip bear-hug. Daniel glanced down in surprise, then lightly patted the top of Todd's head.

Jessie turned to look at her mother. Nancy's lips were slightly pursed. Unable to resist a smug look, Jessie said, "Some parrot, isn't he?"

Before the older woman could form a witty retort, Todd shouted, "Hey, Aunt Jessie!"

"Yes?"

"Could you and Uncle Danny come talk to my class for a show-and-tell?" he asked. "That would be so cool!"

Jessie arched an eyebrow. "Uncle?"

"Well, yeah," the boy replied. "He came with you today, so… I mean…"

"Uh, sure, we'll come speak at your school," she replied, turning beet-red and awkwardly rubbing at the back of her neck, "but he's not your uncle."

"Oh," he said, sounding disappointed. "Okay." He kicked his foot at the dirt, then looked back up. "Are you gonna bring him again at Easter? I bet he's great at finding Easter eggs!"

*****

"All right, students, let's all give our undivided attention to Officer Jessie Parker and her rather *unique* partner," said Mrs. McKelvy. The short, bespectacled matron of Todd Parker's fifth grade class moved aside and smiled at her two esteemed guests.

Jessie stepped forward, took a deep breath, and quickly swept her eyes across the room. "So," she began, "who can tell me what the acronym AO stands for in the Florenceville Police Department?"

Todd's hand immediately shot up. He wiggled it around for good measure.

"*Besides* my nephew," she added, giving him a pointed look that would have been a little more intimidating had it not been accompanied by a smirk.

A few more students raised their hands a bit more calmly while others shared looks of befuddlement. Jessie picked one at random and pointed to her first.

"Android officer?" the young girl said hesitantly, half answer and half question.

"That's one interpretation," Jessie responded. "How about you?"

A boy in the fourth row looked surprised and pointed at his chest. Jessie smiled and nodded. He answered, "Auto... uh, auto... mated officer."

"Automated officer, yes, I've heard that one too," she said. "Anyone else?"

"Artificial officer!" blurted someone from the back row.

Mrs. McKelvy aimed an irritated glare at the student. "Remember: do not answer unless you've been called on."

"Sorry!"

Jessie chuckled. "Very good, kids," she said, "and you're all correct in a way. All three titles have been used at one point or another, although the most commonly referenced one is 'artificial officer'. That's what the news always uses, if you've listened to any broadcasts." She paused for a moment and glanced at Daniel. "Most of us in the force serving with them prefer to use 'android officer' when referencing our partners, though."

"Why?" asked a girl in the third row.

Jessie paused for a moment, considering. She had to keep in mind that she was addressing a group of kids that were only ten or eleven years old. Many of the issues surrounding the still relatively new AO program were rather complex and existential.

"Well," she finally said, "the term 'artificial' implies something that is false or unnatural. And while it's certainly true that our android partners are not natural to this world – they are produced in factories – we're discovering that they aren't completely... Well, think about your computers here at home or in this classroom."

Some of the students glanced towards the desktops at the computer station.

"You see those as tools, right?" Jessie continued. "You don't see them express emotions or have preferences. You don't see them react to pain. And while all those things are not quite the same to androids as they are to us, they still have some range of it. They aren't human, but they're not completely machines either. They're... they're like something in between."

While a few of the students gave contemplative looks or nodded their heads, many others appeared confused and a few shuffled their feet in boredom. Daniel's eyes met Jessie's and a silent message passed between them.

"But enough of all that boring stuff, right?" Jessie said, changing gears and putting a little more pep and bounce in her voice to wake the kids back up. "You guys didn't invite us to hear me drone on. You want to hear from the android, don't you?"

A chorus of positive replies rose up from the children.

"Okay, then," Jessie laughed. "Without further ado, this is my partner. His designation is AO-23, but his friends know him better as Officer Daniel Jones."

The android gave the class a small wave and smiled. "So," he began, "who has questions?"

Nearly every hand in the room immediately shot up. Daniel's eyes widened and he gave a quick, furtive glance to Jessie. She smirked back at him, then turned and helped him out by pointing to the students one at a time to ask their questions.

"What does the twenty-three in your name mean?"

"It means I was the twenty-third android officer produced by that particular factory," he answered.

"How did you end up with your other name?" asked a new student.

"All of the androids at our station carry the surname of Jones because it is common and easy to remember," he began. "The human officers gave us our first names. I am not really sure if there was a particular method to it, though. It may have been in the same way you name your pets."

"There was a method to the madness," Jessie added. "Daniel, Michael, Franklin, Theodore, Edward, and Nicholas. Think about what we usually call you guys when we're being less-than-serious."

He gave her a curious look. "Danny, Mikey, Frankie, Teddy, Eddie, and... Nickster," he rattled off. "Why not Nicky?"

"That was all Pittman's fault," she answered. "He wanted it to be a sort of non-conformist thing."

"Odd," mused Daniel. "Nicholas has always wondered about that. Next question?"

More hands went up and, once again, Jessie helped him by being the mediator.

"What do you eat?"

"The short answer is not much," he said with a soft chuckle. Then, he pulled two items out of the backpack Jessie had brought: one was an orange water bottle and the other was a wrapped, rectangular bar, not that dissimilar from a granola bar in general shape and size. "Once a day, usually before our recharge cycle – that is a lot like how you sleep – we drink one of these bottles to replace any coolant fluids we have lost. Twice a day, we eat one of these bars. That gives us all the fuel and nutrients we need to function, but they are not very tasty."

"You can taste?"

"Sure we can," said Daniel, "although I do not believe that was necessarily an intended effect during programming, but rather more of an oddity that occurred. At any rate, people thought we did not have that sense. Or if they thought we did, they simply assumed we did not care. That is not entirely inaccurate. We would still eat the bars as needed. But, as it stands, we tend to dress them up. It all started when one of the human officers, Biggs, remarked on how dry they look. He tossed a ketchup packet at his partner, Theodore, and that is where it all began." He chuckled. "I am more a fan of peanut butter myself."

"That orange bottle," one of the students inquired, "does that have anything to do with why your badge has orange in it?"

Daniel nodded, glancing between his badge and his partner's. The silver shields looked nearly identical, save for a thick band of color circling the inner emblem of Florenceville – hers was a blue band and his was orange.

"In a way," he answered. "Blue has long been associated with the police force, so most of the badges you see will have that blue band like Officer Jessie's does. All of the android officers are distinguished by our orange bands. That is the same color as our fluids or, if we are hurt and leaking, people associate that as being our blood."

"So," one wide-eyed child asked, "you really do feel pain? Even though you're not human?"

"After a fashion, yes," Daniel said. "I am not entirely sure if it is in the same way that you feel pain, but it is definitely not a pleasant sensation on our end."

"Does that mean you feel emotions, too?"

The android turned his head for a moment in thought. "I believe so," he finally replied. "I know contentment. I know that if a criminal threatens my partner, I get angry and feel a little frightened inside. Those sorts of feelings. From my observation, they do not seem so different from yours."

Right as Jessie pointed at the next student with his hand raised, a blood-curdling scream erupted from a neighboring classroom. Just as quickly, it became muffled. Daniel and Jessie shared a look, then both shot towards the door.

"No," Daniel said, grabbing his partner's arm and holding her back. "Stay here and keep the children safe. Alert the station. I will go investigate."

She glared at him, clearly not agreeing with the idea, but a quick glance back at her frightened nephew made it hard for her to argue. Jessie nodded, and Daniel rushed out of the classroom.

*****

In the hallway, there were no signs of movement or recent activity. The android's eyes carefully swept back and forth, taking in his surroundings. The corridor was relatively short and ended by emptying into an adjoining hallway. Six doors leading to classrooms appeared along both walls, all shut and giving no clue as to which room was in danger.

As Daniel drew his pistol, the third door on the left opened. He took aim, but quickly pointed his muzzle at the ground when he saw it was a teacher's head emerging. She looked around inquisitively, then gasped when she saw him. Daniel put a finger to his lips, and she nodded and ducked back inside the classroom, quietly shutting the door.

The officer carefully approached the first door on his right. He positioned himself against the wall and slowly leaned over to peek in through the glass window. Students sat looking around nervously as their teacher stood protectively between the first row of desks and the door. Daniel locked eyes with him and the teacher shook his head, pointing to the right as if indicating the scream had come from further down the hall and not his room. Daniel nodded and kept moving.

At the sudden sound of muffled crying, the android was able to quickly pinpoint the exact room and hurried down the hall. Again, he positioned himself along the wall right beside the door. He grabbed the doorknob as quietly and carefully as possible. Then, in one swift motion, he turned the knob, shouldered the door open, and raised his weapon.

"Everybody freeze!" he shouted.

A quick visual assessment of the room told Daniel that there were twenty children – all around Todd's age – glued to their seats, terrified. Some had their arms over their heads, others were covering their ears and squeezing their eyes closed, and the rest openly gaped with wide eyes and open mouths.

Directly in front of him stood who he presumed was their teacher. She struggled against a man hidden behind her. He had one arm firmly wrapped around her midsection to keep her trapped while the other held a gun to her head. He was careful to stay ducked down behind her, giving the android no clear shot on him.

"How the hell did you get here so fast?" the armed stranger asked, apparently believing he should've had more time to complete his plans before expecting the police to arrive. "Did you know I was coming?" he shouted at the frightened woman. "Did you warn them?"

"No," she cried, shaking her head and swallowing a tearful sob. "No, I never thought I'd see you again."

"Drop your weapon," Daniel ordered.

"I bet that thought made you happy, huh, bitch?" he roared. "I got fired because of you and your complaint!"

"I said," repeated Daniel, more sternly and loudly, "drop your weapon and let her go."

"Mr. Brown," a student pleaded, "please don't hurt Miss Jackson."

"Can it, kid!" he shouted, brandishing the weapon at the ducking students. "Unless you want me to teach you a lesson after I teach her one!"

Daniel felt fear and frustration coil inside him and he ground his jaws together. The situation was escalating, but Brown was doing a good job of staying tucked behind his hostage. There was no way for the android to shoot him without shooting through her, and attempting any sudden moves in their direction was liable to set the man off.

"Why are you doing this?" he asked, trying a different approach.

"What do you care?!"

"If I know your motive," Daniel reasoned, "then perhaps I can speak with the hostage negotiator for you when he arrives."

"Hostage negotiator?" The man spat. "I'm not stupid. I know how this ends and it isn't with me alive. But at least I can take her with me!" He pulled the hammer back.

"Then at least satisfy my curiosity?" the android asked in a rush.

"Again, why do you care?" Brown asked, enunciating every word as if losing his patience. "You're a robot. It's nothing you would understand anyway."

Daniel cocked his head.

"Like I said, I'm not stupid," the man explained, reading the officer's unasked question on his face. "I can see your orange badge. So, I know you wouldn't understand what it's like to love a woman. And then be rejected by her over and over again. And then get fired because of her!" He tugged against Jackson, causing her to cry out in fear.

"You underestimate me," Daniel replied. "I actually do know what it is like to love a woman. She has not rejected me, however, so perhaps I am simply more of a man than you."

Brown lost his temper and roared. He turned Jackson away so he could have a clear view of the android before pulling the trigger – which was exactly what Daniel had hoped for when he baited the man. Five shots rang out. The classroom filled with shrieks and screams. Brown's body, with one bullet through the forehead, collapsed to the ground in front of the teacher's desk.

Daniel blinked and looked down. Four holes bleeding orange from his stomach greeted him. A stomach that would have been protected had he not continuously turned Jessie down when she offered him her back-up vest, he thought with a grim amount of humor. The humor quickly died when the pain struck him. He fell to his knees. A single bullet in the back of the shoulder had been one thing, a fairly manageable situation all around. Multiple bullets in the midsection, where lots of important parts were gathered, were not nearly as agreeable. It hurt. A *lot*. And the world was suddenly moving very slowly.

Lying down seemed like a good idea, so Daniel sank onto his back while clutching his wounds. The lights were entirely too bright. He squinted. Then he heard someone shout his name. Entirely too loudly. But he could not squint his ears.

Jessie's face came into view. Daniel smiled. He had always found her aesthetically pleasing, especially on the inside, though perhaps that was not the proper phrasing. He had never told her. He was not sure why he had refrained, now that he pondered it, although he supposed it was because he had not felt it was his place to do so. What an odd time to have such thoughts. The combination of the severe damage and the fire of pain were clearly making his cognitive faculties go haywire. *Is this what it is like for humans when they are dying?* he wondered.

His partner looked very upset, probably because of him. Daniel felt guilty. He glanced away and saw her hands on top of his, all covered in orange everywhere. When he looked back up, he saw she was trying to get his attention. His brows knitted together as he focused on listening as hard as his present condition would allow.

"Danny? Can you hear me, sweetie?"

"Hmmm?" he hummed at her in response.

"They're almost here and they've got Gerald with them," she said hurriedly. "You're gonna be okay, just please hold on. Stay with me. Please."

Daniel tried to say something, but ended up coughing instead. He tasted coolant in his mouth. That seemed like a bad thing.

Tears rolled down Jessie's face. She lowered her head down until her forehead brushed against his. "Stay with me, Danny," she whispered, soft and pleading. "I love you. Please, stay."

Her hands were on top of his. Daniel slowly turned his so that their palms met. And then he squeezed her hands. He heard her breath hitch right before the sound of sirens drowned out all the rest.

Epilogue

"What makes a man?" Captain Tinnerman asked rhetorically, addressing the gathered crowd in a very solemn voice. "How do we measure him? Centuries ago, it was by whether or not he owned land. A hundred years ago, it was by the color of his skin. Decades ago, it was by the gender of whom he loved.

"And now? Is it by biology, by anatomy, by how he came into this world? Or is it, perhaps, something more? A mindset. A belief. One's own sense of self and place in the world. How he treats others. How he carries himself. How he perceives himself and how others perceive him. What he's willing to sacrifice to keep others safe. These all seem more pertinent to me than what someone's body possesses or from where their life originated."

He paused, eyes skimming the room, and then continued. "Last week, we came within a hair's breadth of losing a very good man. Not because he was brave enough to risk his life protecting a classroom full of innocent children and their teacher from a gun-wielding madman, but because we failed him. As a police department, we failed to give him the very basic of protections that we afford our human officers. Why? Because we considered the android officers as lesser. Less than men. Less, even, than our canine units. No more."

Captain Tinnerman turned to his left and looked at Daniel and Jessie standing side by side on the stage with him. He then turned to his right and smiled at the tall, portly fellow by his side. "Thanks in part to a very generous budget increase from our mayor, as well as an outpouring of donations from the general public after the news story first broke, I am happy to announce that all of our android officers have now been outfitted with bullet-proof vests."

He waited for the smattering of applause to die down before continuing. "I would also like to announce that as of today, the Florenceville Police Department shall no longer make a distinction between our android officers and our human officers. As far as I am concerned, they are as precious, as valuable, and as irreplaceable as our natural-born personnel and will henceforth be treated as such.

"Their orange badges have been replaced with traditional blue ones and we will no longer make distinctions between our officers when speaking with the press. To aid in this matter, they are now allowed to pick a surname of their own choosing rather than being assigned 'Jones'. Those wishing to retain 'Jones' are, of course, more than welcome to do so."

He paused briefly, waiting once again as more applause followed.

"And now, without further ado, it is my distinct honor to bestow upon Officer Daniel Parker our highest award: the Star of Valor."

Captain Tinnerman then turned to his left and pinned a small silver star to the right lapel of the android's uniform. As the crowd raucously applauded and the flashbulbs of reporters lit up the room, Jessie smiled at Daniel as he squeezed her hand.

The Lady and the Dragon

Written by

T. M. Lowe

"D RAGON!"

I open my eyes and raise my head, looking around quickly. Nothing but chewed-up bones and my hoard of trinkets and shiny baubles. At least the humans aren't in my cave; not yet, but they're close. Stupid. I shake my head. How had I not heard or smelled them approaching? Must be getting longer in the tooth more quickly than I thought. Disappointing.

"Dragon!" the voice shouts again, then says some other things that I don't quite understand.

I sigh. I don't want to fight these people. I want to be left alone. In peace. But it's the same story every time: find a suitable living space, start acquiring treasure, then the humans come moving in. Once you start snatching a cow or sheep or two – or several – they start getting uppity about it. I was here first. You move!

The rabble rousing starts getting louder outside the cave entrance. This is clearly not going away on its own, and I realize I'm stalling. Fine. Okay.

Time to deal with it. I take a deep breath through my mouth rather than my nostrils, filling my fire lung in preparation for a fight.

I step outside and immediately make myself look as big and intimidating as possible, spreading my wings out to their full span. My neck frill puffs out and rattles against the horns on my jawline, making an audible warning sound for the gathered humans. I bare my teeth at them, smoky tendrils wafting up between the spaces.

And that's when I realize that not a one of these people has a weapon on them.

The humans babble and scream incoherently. Most of them turn tail and run back down the mountain path. A few turn and accidentally run into each other before gathering themselves up and following their brethren back to the town in the foothills.

One human remains, though it is not by choice. A young woman, with hair as fiery red as my scales, stands before me, tied to a length of wood hastily planted into the ground. She looks up at me with green eyes and is clothed in the same shade of emerald. To her credit, she isn't crying. She doesn't even look that frightened, actually. More defiant than anything. Like she's daring me to eat her or something. She bites down on the strip of cloth in her mouth as if it's some sort of challenge.

I like her spunk already.

But, seriously, what fresh sorcery is this? I've been run out of a few homes in my time, but it usually involved folks in metal with sharp, pointy objects. This is... Well, this is something altogether odd and new for me. Were the villagers trying to placate me or something? Here, eat this random lady and leave our livestock alone! I can only imagine the sordid thought process involved in all this.

However, I can't dwell on that thought any longer. I've been holding my fire inside all this time and it's got to come out some way or another. I turn my head to the side and release it with a bellowing roar. Whew. That's much better.

When I look back to the human, she appears a little more frightened now.

I fold my neck frill and wings back in, sitting back on my haunches and hoping to appear less fearsome. I have zero desire to consume this woman. I ate a knight once, after I managed to pry that annoying metal shell off, and I found the meat far too gamey and gristly for my preference. Also tore my innards up something fierce. Never again.

However, I do notice something sparkly on her forehead. Looks like some sort of tiara, perhaps. I reach down slowly, so as not to frighten her any more than she already is, and carefully pluck it off her head with the claws on my thumb and index finger. I hold the treasure up and carefully inspect it. It's quite a nice piece: solid gold circlet with a raised knot pattern at the front with gemstones embedded at the points, one ruby, one emerald, and one... is that a diamond? I think it is. Oh, lovely, that will look divine in my hoard.

She looks up at me and tries to babble something through the gag. I've no idea what she's saying. I haven't exactly had any need or interest in learning the humans' tongue. In fact, it's been my general goal to avoid them as much as possible, but they keep finding ways of intruding. I recognize "yes," "no," and "dragon," and that's about the extent of my knowledge. The fact that her mouth is impeded by the cloth makes it even less likely that I'll recognize any words.

Instead, my interest in the situation wanes and I step back inside my cave to deposit my new acquisition. There, right atop the stack of gold coins will do nicely.

Dusk approaches and hunger grows in the pit of my stomach. Since the townsfolk have obviously tried to appease me by offering up this poor soul bound outside my cave, I decide to leave their livestock be for the night and manage to take down a buck near the outskirts of the forest. I bring it back to my mountaintop home clutched in my jaws, eyeing the maiden as I pass by. Her head suddenly bobs up as if waking and watches me closely. I do not stop and head inside to have my meal.

Shortly after finishing supper, I hear a muted scream and barking. I rush outside, all tense muscle and building flame, to see a pack of wild dogs surrounding the woman tied to the stake. They are menacing her and she's understandably fearful. I probably should not have left her tied up out here, but I didn't really know what to do. I've never been given a hostage before. I don't know how this is all supposed to work. It's *awkward*, okay?

So, I do the first thing that comes to mind: I protect her. I snap my jaws shut around the first dog that lunges at her and give it a violent shake, breaking its back. The next to launch itself towards her gets hurled against a pine tree courtesy of my right front talon. The other four dogs begin to back away, snarling and snapping. They're hungry and the trapped girl is easy prey, but they're now unsure it is worth the risk to fight me for her.

I make their decision easy for them by planting myself firmly between the dogs and the woman, spreading my wings, and roaring at the pack with the full force of my lungs. I am dragon, the apex predator, and I am all that is might! With a whimper of defeat, the canines tuck tail and retreat off into the cover of the coniferous forest.

I smile, rather pleased with myself, and puff my chest up as I turn to glance down at the woman. *Aren't you impressed?* my expression asks. Her face is unreadable at first, which vexes me. I'm not sure why I care what this stranger thinks, but to be honest, I rarely have witnesses to my prowess that live to tell the tale, so this is a new and rather exciting experience. She looks at me, then off towards where the dogs disappeared and back to me again. She smiles and says something that I assume to be thanks or gratitude. I bobble my shoulders and give her a little warbling trill, sufficiently pleased. She laughs at that.

Gently, I pluck the stake out of the ground and carry her inside my cave, safe from the dark night and the predators that stalk it. I tear her rope bindings with my claws and she slips free of them, reaching up to pull the cloth gag from her mouth.

She babbles at me again and I turn my head at an angle to look down at her, trying to convey that I don't speak her language. I am unsure if she takes that gesture as some sort of response to her words, but suddenly she wraps her arms around my right front leg and presses her face against my scales. I stiffen, trying hard not to outright recoil. Ew. Ew. Ew. I don't like being touched, *especially* by something that doesn't also have scales. We dragons are very much loners, for the most part. We seek out our own secluded dwelling places and only gather when it's time to ensure the continuation of the species. Otherwise, we much prefer to simply be left alone to our hunting and our hoards, thank you very much.

Thankfully, the young woman releases me and I try to settle back down. I watch as she carefully looks around my cave, slowly moving around to find her bearings. It's only then that I realize her human eyes may be having trouble seeing. There is a bit of moonlight still shining in through the entrance which is just fine for my vision, but it may be too dark for hers. I sigh, then grab the wooden stake she'd been tied to previously. I break it in half, suck in a quick breath, and light the wood on fire. There. A nice little campfire in the middle of my cave. That's going to bugger my sinuses for a while, so I hope she's happy that I'm taking this much effort to make her comfortable here.

That leads me to a troubling thought: just how long is she staying here? I've never been in this situation before. What does one do with a maiden if they don't make a meal of them? I'm at a loss. I suppose she can't simply return to the village from whence she came; they sacrificed her to me, after all, so I guess they won't be taking her back anytime soon. Should I find another village and just, I don't know, drop her off? A little flyby drop-and-go? Do humans take in other humans like that? Maybe she'll wander off by morning and find a new home, thus solving my problem. She's certainly not my prisoner, by any means.

The woman seems pleased with my fire and sits down beside it, holding her hands up and rubbing them together quickly. She looks over and up at me and I return her gaze. I suppose the company isn't so bad, but this feels rather awkward, two individuals sitting together who can't speak the same language and share nothing in common.

She apparently feels the same and is the first to break the uncomfortable silence. She places her left hand on her chest and says, "Aideen."

I blink at her.

The maiden repeats, "Aideen." She pats her chest a few times. "I am Aideen."

The brow ridges above my eyes furrow down as I frown. I don't know what she's expecting from me. Our vocal chords and lips are not the same. I cannot hope to form her speech on my own tongue. I cannot say her name. And if she expects me to tell her mine, she'll be sorely disappointed. I don't have one. None of us do. It's not a thing dragons recognize. We are who we are. No label is required to distinguish this, especially when interactions are few and far between. We don't exactly gossip about one another like a flock of birds would.

Once again, she looks at me rather expectantly and slowly enunciates, "Ai-deen."

I crinkle my nostrils at her. Fine. She wants to pursue this madness, why not? I clear my throat and make an attempt. "A-a-a-e-e-e-e-e."

Her eyes light up.

I frown. Now that I've tried it, the name shouldn't be too hard for me to manage. It's mostly guttural throat sounds, but the second half was off. I try again, this time placing my tongue against the back of my teeth for the beginning and end of that second syllable. "Ai-i-i-i-d-e-e-e-e-en," I slowly croak.

The woman gasps, covering her nose and mouth with her hands momentarily before bringing them back down and clapping them together. "Yes," she shouts, "yes!"

I cock my head at her. I have no idea what this exercise is about, unless she doubted my intelligence. Which I suppose is a possibility. Perhaps she thought me just another simple, mindless beast until I'd shown otherwise by choosing to save her from the wild dogs. Maybe she's trying to see if there is more than simply a wild animal in me.

The lady then removes her hand from her chest and stretches it out towards me, pointing her index finger at my own scaled chest. "You?" she says with an upward inflection at the end, designating it is a question directed towards me.

Well, now, she's just taught me a new human word. The problem is that I don't have a sufficient answer for her. I have no name. So, I try to say the human word that I know for such a response. I place my tongue against the back of my teeth again – very awkward – because I recognize their "n" sound requires it. "No," I say, and I accompany it with a shake of my head, which I also recognize as a non-verbal symbol of the word.

She frowns. I hope she doesn't take my response as a refusal to disclose such information. I simply don't have any to give. Aideen gives me a thoughtful look for several moments before her face lights up. "Pestifar," she says.

Come again?

"You," she points at my chest once more, "Pestifar."

Huh. It seems Aideen has decided to give me a name. Well, then, it's better than nothing, I suppose. I don't rightly care one way or the other, but if she feels that I need one for her own benefit, so be it. I smile and give her a sagely nod. She looks satisfied.

Awkward silence follows once more. This is a bit irritating, as I am used to simply being alone with my own thoughts. With someone else around, I feel as if I should be doing something or acting in some way. It's uncomfortable, like I'm not even in my own cave anymore. Humph.

As I rap my claws on the stone floor, I notice Aideen shooting furtive glances towards the picked-over deer I'd eaten earlier in the evening. Ah, yes, I hadn't thought of that before now. She spent the day tied up. Who knows when she last had a meal? And she's either being polite or careful – or both – by leaving my kill alone.

I reach over to the carcass, wrench loose a remaining leg, and attempt to hand it to her. The woman's eyes widen and she leans back in disgust, staring at the blood dripping from the end of the rump. For a moment, I'm confused by her reaction. Didn't she want some of this food a moment ago? Clearly I was giving my permission by offering it to her, wasn't I?

Aideen must see the questions reflected in my expression because she makes it a point to look at the leg, look at the fire, then look back to me. I connect the dots quickly and feel slightly foolish. I don't make it a habit to pass by humans very often, but I recall times when I had and saw them roasting their food on a campfire. I look at our small, dinky one and chirp a laugh. That thing wouldn't cook a skinny rat. I can do her one better.

My fire's much hotter, more concentrated. I flash her a toothy grin, suck in a deep breath, hold the leg in front of my snout, and engulf the meat in swirling flame. I notice her gasp and look at my talon in worry. That's kind of her, but there is no need for concern. Dragons are born of fire, we live it and it lives within us. A dragon's fire is our defense against all other threats that *aren't* our own kind. Flame does nothing to our scales.

After my first breath runs out, I sniff the rump. It still has a bloody scent, so I roast it again. Once it no longer smells raw, I give it a moment to cool off, then hand it back to Aideen. She gifts me with a thankful smile and I answer with a bobble of my shoulders and warbling trill, like earlier. We may not speak the language, but I think we're starting to work out a means of communication, no less.

When she finishes eating, she sets the buck leg aside and looks around with her hands held mid-air. Then, with a heavy sigh, she wipes them clean on the bottom of her green dress. I yawn and stretch my front legs out while arching my back slightly. It's been a long, rather eventful day. I see that Aideen feels similarly as she stretches her arms to the side and yawns as well.

I give the campfire an extended blow of air and manage to snuff most of it out, leaving only a pile of glowing embers. That will do. I need as much darkness as possible to sleep well. I settle into my favorite spot in the cave and drift into slumber.

Something touches me. My eyes snap open. It's still dark, so I have no idea how long I've been asleep. The young woman is now leaning against my left side, shivering. She must be cold. I shiver, too, but not because I'm cold. Like before, feeling her skin against my scales makes my skin crawl, like I'm being infested with parasites. I don't mean her offense. She seems like a nice girl. I just simply can't abide this odd feeling and texture. I'll never get back to sleep like this.

Hoping not to disturb her slumber, I slowly slide away from Aideen so that we're no longer pressed against each other. When I hear no protests, I assume that I'm in the clear. However, I don't wish for her to feel cold, so I stretch my left wing out and lower it down as much as possible, resting the tip against the floor and creating a sort of low-hung tent canopy for her. Hopefully, that will help trap any warm air in and keep her comfortable without us needing to touch.

I start to rise from the fog of sleep when the sunlight streaming through the cave entrance hits my face. I open my eyes and look under my wing. Aideen is still there, but already awake. She looks up at me with a small smile. I give her a short, soft trill before standing up and stretching out my legs and wings. She repeats a similar motion and looks up at me expectantly - which feels odd because I don't know how humans actually live nor what their daily routine is. I can't imagine it's identical to a dragon's.

Regardless, if her prerogative is to follow my lead, I have no problem going about my day. I chirp at her and motion my head towards the cave entrance, trying to give her a sign that clearly indicates she should come with me. It must have gotten the message across as I notice her following me outside. Good.

I lead her to a nearby mountain stream and dip my head down for a cool, refreshing drink. From the corner of my eye, I watch her scoop water into her hands and bring it up to her face to drink, then she splashes it over her face and neck. Once I've had my fill, I look over to her. When she looks up at me, I hold my left talon out and up at her to indicate she should stay while I go off alone. Thankfully, it seems she understands that symbol and I quickly steal away out of sight to relieve myself.

When I return to where I left Aideen, she resumes her place by my side and we walk back to my cave together. With daylight illuminating the interior, my treasure hoard truly looks gorgeous. My eyes sweep over the gold and silver piles, filled with various coins and jewels from my travels, and take in the way they glint and sparkle. From the corner of my eye, I see Aideen equally admiring my collection with a smile upon her face. I am torn between feeling proud that she likes my hoard and feeling defensive that she may try to pocket an item.

She suddenly gasps and I watch as she runs towards one of the piles and looks closely. Then, she picks up the circlet I took from her and places it upon her head. I see nothing but red. I rush forward, growling at her and barely containing my rage. Had this been some strange interloper, I'd have roasted them where they stood. Instead, I try and restrain myself as best I can since this woman didn't exactly choose to be stuck with me. But that trinket is *mine* now, no longer hers. That's how ownership works. And I chose to take it rather than her life, which is what her fellow humans had offered up to me, so she should be *grateful* that's all I am interested in.

Aideen's eyes widen. She quickly removes the headpiece and tosses it back onto the pile. Then, she backs away from me until she bumps into the wall of my cave. The woman cowers, looking up at me in fear. The red drains from my vision and I give my head a quick shake, sitting back on my haunches.

I feel terrible. I... I hadn't meant to terrify her so. I still mean her no harm. I'd just wanted her to leave my possessions alone. That's my hoard, only I should touch it. Maybe humans operate differently and this is a cultural misunderstanding. Either way, she's still acting frightened and I don't know how to make things better. I also feel rather embarrassed. Perhaps I overreacted, I don't know. I need to clear my head and food would be a good idea as well, so I turn and leave the cave.

The weather is beautiful for flying today, which pleases me immensely. I get a running start, spread my wings, and leap off the mountaintop. It feels good to flex my muscles and I beat a steady rhythm until I find those delicious thermals of hot air near the coastline. There, I can simply keep my wings extended and glide along playfully. The salty sea air feels good for my soul as I breathe in deeply, enjoying the peace of watching the waves crash against the shore below me. A few terns join my dance in the air and I chuckle at them.

Before I head back, I make a pass along the road that the humans often use. My diligence is soon rewarded in the form of a trader's covered cart plodding along the pathway. I fold my wings tight against my sides and swoop down. The man and ox are caught unawares and I quickly snap the animal's neck to prevent it from bolting. The human screams, jumps off his cart, and runs into the woods. I let him go. I'm much more interested in his ox and make a quick meal of it. After I've had my fill, I leave the rest for the lesser beasts of the land.

The wooden cart is heavy and rather awkward to clutch in my front talons, but it's bound to contain some sort of treasure to add to my hoard. If not, then at the very least, it may have some items useful to Aideen. Once I have a good hold on it, I beat my wings hard and finally get airborne. It's a bit of a struggle, but my cave isn't too far. I am relieved to drop my burden outside the cave entrance upon my return.

But something isn't right. I smell a strange dragon. Then, I hear Aideen scream from the back of my cave. I rush in with a roar, neck frill fully extended and rattling dangerously.

The intruder is a blue-scaled male who has Aideen cornered against the far wall. He spins around with eyes wide and immediately makes a submissive showing, crouching down against the floor and turning his head so that his neck is exposed to me. He looks up with an apologetic expression.

"I'm sorry, I'm sorry!" he cries at me.

I growl at him. "Why are you in my cave, Blue?"

His eyes glance about nervously. It makes me angrier.

"You can't possibly have thought it abandoned because my scent is strong here. Tell me why you are trespassing or I'll rip out your throat!"

"I, well, you see, I," he sputters. What a craven, sniveling coward. "I was in the area and noticed the human scent and thought maybe—"

"—Maybe what? That she'd slain me?"

"Well, maybe not so much," he responds, "but I thought I might help you out with your little problem."

What is this idiot on about? "And what problem might that be, Blue?"

He side-eyes Aideen. "Is she a princess?"

What? "I have no idea. How should I know? And what does it matter?"

"Princesses are nothing but trouble for dragons," he claims. "I've heard tales of knights and princes slaying dragons because of them."

This is ridiculous. Blue has obviously been mixing about with human stories too much. It's affecting his brain. "I highly doubt she'll be trouble. Her people rejected her, left her outside my cave as an offering."

"Oh," he says, looking rather deflated, "but she still may be dangerous. I could... you know... take care of that for you."

I don't like the way he leers at her. I especially don't like the way he licks his chops, either.

"Leave now or I kill you." I rattle my neck frills against my jaw horns loudly as I glare down at him.

"Red, you should really reconsider—"

"LEAVE! I will not ask kindly again!"

Blue's feet scatter almost comically as he scrambles around me and out of my cave. I rush behind him and roar at his fleeing form for good measure, making sure I've gotten my point across sufficiently.

"And I have a name! It's Pestifar!"

My skin suddenly crawls as I feel the woman wrap her arms around my right foreleg. I hear her whisper the name she's given me as she touches her forehead against my arm. I look down at her and whimper, trying to delicately tug myself out of her grasp. I'm almost positive this is some sort of pleasing gesture in her world, but I just cannot abide the physical feeling of it.

Aideen lets go and looks up at me with a confused expression and sad eyes. I feel incredibly awkward. Here she was trying to express gratitude, I'm guessing, and I've rebuked her, hurt her feelings. I sigh heavily, unsure of how to communicate the issue. But if we're going to be around each other long-term at all, she has got to understand or I'll go mad.

I look down at her and give a soft, sad warble. Then, an idea hits me and I turn to face her directly. I gently grab her arm, which is covered by the long sleeves of her green dress. I rub the cloth against the back of my other talon and nod my head at her with a smile. Her eyebrows pull together. I brace myself, then move her arm so that her bare hand rubs against my talon. I shudder slightly and shake my head with a frown. I release her arm.

Aideen's face appears thoughtful for a few moments before she looks up at me and nods. Oh, thank mercy. Hopefully she understands what I was trying to convey. With that now behind us, I gesture my head towards the outside of my cave and go out to where I'd dropped the cart. She follows me.

The young lady helps me pull back the canvas topper from the cart and together we start picking through the haul. There is a wide variety of various sundry items, along with food preserved in jars and such that hold no interest for me, but it's good they are there for Aideen. I highly doubt a carnivore's diet would be suitable for her for any length of time.

Where I am less than excited about the overall goods, the woman appears beside herself with happiness, so I'm glad I dragged that heavy load back. I watch as she pulls out a blanket and lays it on the ground beside the cart, then begins to pile items onto it. A few more folded blankets are tossed onto it, several books, the jars of food, and some objects I can't identify. She pulls out a sword and looks it over with wide eyes, then gives it a few awkward swings.

I grumble. The sight of the weapon makes me uneasy, even though I know she means me no harm with it.

Aideen glances up at me, then puts the sword back in the cart. She next pulls out a small dagger and it fits her hand much better than the sword did.

She adds it to her little pile. The dagger doesn't bother me so much given its relative size. In fact, I'm actually rather happy she's got something besides me to help defend herself when needed.

The woman's eyes light up suddenly and she pulls one final item from the cart: a set of gloves. She quickly pulls them onto both her hands and looks up at me. Ah, I see where this is going now. Aideen approaches me, holds her gloved hands out, and catches my eyes with her own as if asking for permission. I give her a small nod and hold my breath as she reaches out to stroke my chest. To my surprise, it's not so bad; not any worse than the feel of her dress. She babbles to me, I assume a question. I give her a soft trilling sound in response, nodding once. She smiles deeply.

I help the lady drag her blanket of goodies inside my cave and leave the unwanted items in the cart outside. She busies herself with sorting through her little pile.

Meanwhile, I walk over to my treasure hoard and settle down beside it. I reach out and dip both talons deep into a pile of gold coins and watch how they sparkle and shine. I pull up fistfuls and release them to fall back down into the pile, relishing the tinkling sound they make as they cascade around. I grab another handful of coins and make a fist, massaging them around with my fingers. Now *this* is the sort of texture I enjoy feeling and it takes me to a happy place in my mind.

"Pestifar?"

I glance up at Aideen's voice, slightly irritated at having my revelry interrupted. She points to the wall behind her and I find myself slightly taken aback. There are suddenly pictures that were not there before. I walk over and sit down beside her, taking the scene in. She's painted some sort of story about our adventures together thus far. There is a red dragon, which I presume to be my representation, that looks big, strong, and valiant standing protectively in front of a small caricature of Aideen. In front of my character, an evil-looking blue dragon and the pack of wild dogs are drawn running away from me in terror. I chuckle.

"Pestifar," Aideen says, drawing my attention back down to her. She says two nonsense words to me, but she draws them out very slowly and enunciates carefully. She must be trying to teach me more of her language and it seems very important to her. She says them again and I frown, cocking my head. I'm trying, Aideen, I really am.

The lady points to the picture she's drawn of me defending her, then crosses her hands over the left side of her chest and repeats the two words. "Thank. You." She points to the items she took from the cart I'd brought back, repeats the hand-crossing motion on her chest, and says, less slowly, "Thank you."

I think I understand now. Some sort of expression of gratitude. I slowly nod at her, but I should probably show my understanding in a clearer manner. So, I attempt to show my own gratitude by mimicking the very human action of which she seems so fond: I wrap a talon around her and draw her to my chest. Aideen is cognizant enough to place a gloved hand between her face and my scales as I do this, and I can't help but smile. She giggles happily and repeats my name a few times. I do believe we're making progress in this whole communication challenge.

When I let her go, I glance outside and realize more time has passed than I originally thought. Heh. I must've been more entranced by my hoard-musing than usual. But that presents a bit of a problem. The cart contained enough food to probably last Aideen for a little while, but I've still got to eat. And while that little dagger of hers is better defense than nothing, it won't do her a lick of good if that creepy blue scale comes back while I'm gone. I look back and forth between the lady and the cave entrance several times, torn. I'm very, very hesitant to leave her behind again. It was almost disastrous this morning.

It's as if Aideen can read my mind. She goes over to her hoard of items and picks out a blanket and two lengths of rope. She then gestures to me to approach her. I've seen humans riding on horses before, so I already have some idea of what she has in mind. I simply have no idea if it will actually work, though.

I lie down as flat as possible for her. It's a stretch, but she manages to toss the blanket onto my back, just behind my shoulder blades. She tosses one rope over the front of the blanket and one rope over the back end and motions for me to stand. As I do so, Aideen ties the ends of each rope together so that they both fit snugly against my stomach, effectively making a very crude saddle. I lie down once more and let her climb up onto my back. I can feel her tightly tuck her fingers underneath the front rope to make a good grip for herself.

Admittedly, I'm nervous about this idea. I'm going to be constantly distracted by the potential of her getting blown off by the rush of wind. But I don't see a better alternative at the moment, either.

I step out of our cave and decide to test the waters a little more safely first. Normally, I'd take my usual running start and then bound off the mountaintop. Instead, I turn the other direction and follow the pathway at a speedy trot. I glance behind and Aideen gives me a smile. Okay, seems things are good so far. I increase my speed up to a rather fast run. I don't hear her fall off or make any worrying noises.

Running at top speed now, I reach a clearing free of trees and test out a few wing flaps. Aideen gasps and I swivel my head around in a panic, but she's fine. The lady's laughing, actually, so those were apparently sounds of amusement rather than trouble. I take a deep breath through my nostrils and steady my nerves. It's now or never. I start rapidly beating my wings and, within a few moments, my feet lose contact with the ground, so I tuck them up underneath my body.

Aideen makes more sounds of awe and amusement, and I chortle. I make an effort to keep as steady and slow as possible without losing too much air speed to stay aloft. Thankfully, there is a human farm nearby. I carefully swoop in low, grab a sheep before it can flee, and laboriously flap and turn to regain altitude and head home. I check on the young woman again after that particular maneuver, but she's still planted firmly on the blanket saddle with a wide grin plastered across her face. She must love flying as much as I do and this revelation amuses me more than it probably should.

Once back at the cave, Aideen releases the knots on the ropes and frees me of the saddle. I tear off one of the sheep's haunches and hold it towards her to ask if she'd like any, but she shakes her head and goes inside. I make short work of the animal before joining her.

The woman is over in her corner messing about with her jars of food, so I curl up in my usual spot and lie down, settling in for the night. Shortly after, Aideen wanders over with a book and two blankets. She places one blanket partially on the floor and partially against my neck. Then, she takes a seat on the blanket and leans back against me, keeping our contact carefully divided by the cloth.

I smile. She's more thoughtful than I'd have usually given humans credit for.

She places the other blanket over her lap and opens up the book, taking advantage of what little evening light still pours in through the cave entrance. I glance at the cover from the corner of my eye and see a depiction of a dragon battling an armored knight on a horse. The dragon has a spear stuck in its gut.

I shiver.

Aideen reaches out a gloved hand and lightly scratches behind my jawline, and I find it surprisingly soothing. I lean into her touch slightly and close my eyes.

I'm not entirely sure why she stays. She's not my prisoner. She's free to leave at any point in time. Surely there are other humans who would shelter her and they'd probably be much better company than me. But, for whatever reason, she chooses to remain. And I actually like that. I never wanted company before, but now I honestly enjoy it. Heh. Guess I'm going soft with age.

Our days pass by in a nice, familiar pattern. Aideen reads her books and paints more pictures while I gaze at my growing treasure hoard. I keep us fed and bring back the occasional trader caravan for us to sort through. And we go flying together at least twice a day so I can hunt, but sometimes we'll go out and catch a breeze just for the joy of it. We live in the moment, as dragons do, with no thought of the previous days and no worry of the future ones. There is only here and now.

Until the pattern changes. I smell a mix of horse and human approaching our cave. I look over at Aideen. She has no idea that danger is coming. I'm torn. Fight or flee? Protect my hoard and my lady or grab her and run? I glance at the blanket saddle rig in the corner. I have no idea if there's time to put it on before they reach us. But I can't tell from scent alone how many there are and the hoof beats give no clear number.

I make my decision.

Aideen gasps as I grab her up in my right talon and awkwardly bound to the entrance on three legs. Then, she screams as we come screeching to a halt just outside, blocked off by a small army of knights.

I'm too late. I hesitated too long.

Ten armored men sit on armored horses. Nine of them draw their swords. The one in the center with purple feathers atop his helmet bears a lance. I am reminded of Aideen's book cover. I also recall Blue's words about princesses and danger to dragons.

Is Aideen a princess? Is this her prince come to kill me and claim her?

"Dragon!" Feathers shouts at me, then spews a line of human nonsense that I don't understand. He gestures to the lady in my grasp.

I look down at Aideen. There are tears in her eyes. She looks frightened. "Pestifar, no," she says, pointing to Feathers. "No!"

I don't know what she means by that. Is she telling me no because she doesn't want to go with them or telling me not to kill them?

"Aideen!" the prince yells in a very loud and commanding voice, throwing out another tirade of words. It's odd because his tone sounds laced with a threat. But he's addressing her and not me. Seems strange for a supposed rescue party to yell at the person they perceive as kidnapped.

The lady starts trembling in my talon and buries her face against my thumb, sobbing. She repeats my name quietly as if in prayer. In the moment, I don't even think about her flesh pressed against my scales and how that normally bothers me. Instead, I feel a steady rage growing inside. Aideen is clearly frightened not just of this situation but of the prince himself. I suspect there is a history between these two, and it is not a good one. Perhaps this is why she chose to stay with me all this time – she has nothing pleasant to which to return.

I trill at the woman and she looks up at me. I nod, then set her down. The prince beckons to her. Aideen shakes her head and retreats to just inside the cave entrance. He yells at her, gesticulating wildly enough that his horse paws at the ground, agitated.

I give Feathers my most withering glare and position myself between his knights and my lady, hissing loudly.

He doesn't like that very much and gestures to his men.

My wings snap open to either side as my neck frill pulls up and rattles.

One knight loses his nerve and gallops back down the mountain path. Feathers *really* doesn't like that and yells at those who remain.

I pull in a deep breath through my mouth. As the horses charge toward me, I expel a large gout of flame and sidestep their charge. Man and animal scream alike. Four more of my adversaries run back down the pathway, all smoking and scorched flesh. Five remain and I assess their positions. Feathers is hanging back with his lance while the other four have begun to circle me.

I spin, trying to keep all the knights in view. This would be much easier if I went airborne; then I could simply rain down fire upon their heads. As it stands, I worry that one of them may get inside my cave and go after Aideen, so I want to stay between them and her. Unfortunately, that is slightly limiting.

A sword nicks my right rear leg and I lash out with my tail, sending the knight flying into the bushes. His horse runs away in terror. I tense those leg muscles and can feel the wound is not deep. Good.

I swipe a claw at one of the other circling knights, but miss. Another tries to stick his sword in my same wounded leg, but I pull away in time. He pays for it when I snap him up in my jaws and crunch down as hard as possible, then toss his lifeless body away.

I draw in more air and release flames once again. The two remaining knights dance their mounts out of the way. I notice Feathers is still holding back, watching the battle. Coward. Letting his men die for him.

Both knights decide that charging me at the same time from opposite directions is their best bet. And I have to admit, it's a solid plan. For one of them. For the other, it means death in my jaws and I toss his corpse aside before turning my attention to the sword stuck in my tail. I give it a few, firm swings, but the weapon is stuck solid. It's annoying and certainly hurts, but hardly life-threatening, so I turn back around.

The remaining knight grabs my attention as he slides off his horse and runs into my cave. I chase after him, roaring in anger. *Nobody* is touching Aideen on my watch. Not while I still draw breath.

She's backed against the wall screaming when I enter our cavern. The knight has her cornered and turns to face me far too late. I snatch him up in my right talon and squeeze until his shrieking stops and the metal of his armor gives a satisfying snap.

I turn and fling the body out of the cave just in time for the prince's lance to impale my right shoulder as he comes charging in. It sinks in deep until I feel it stop violently against bone. The lance snaps in half and the prince trots his horse around to my other side and disappears from view. I groan in pain. My entire right arm is shooting fire inside and I feel disoriented. Aideen is screaming again.

I'm angry. About everything. The situation. The prince. Myself for letting this happen. I reach up with my left talon and rip the broken lance out, flinging it against the far wall. That does nothing to alleviate the pain. And I may have just made things worse because that is a lot of blood flowing out now. Worrying.

I limp in a circle trying to find this little cretin. His mount goes running out of the cave, whinnying in panic. Feathers isn't on it. He's staying just out of view and the few times I do spot him, he's out of reach. Maddening. I roar my frustration. My foreleg is covered in my blood, dripping down and marking a path everywhere I go. I realize now that Feathers is playing a game with me. Letting me wear myself down and bleed out so that he can swoop in for an easy kill. If Aideen wasn't in here, I'd smother my cave in dragon fire. As it stands, I'm out of options.

And there's nothing I can do about it. The truth hits me hard and I whimper, my injured shoulder buckling on me. I collapse to the floor and hiss as my weight lands on my right shoulder. Grunting, I roll over to my left side and await the end. I'm so sorry, Aideen. I tried my best.

Right on cue, Feathers finally graces my vision with his presence. He saunters up to me, his countenance full of arrogance. He lifts the visor of his helm, locks eyes with mine, and babbles something at me, then laughs. Something mocking, I'm sure. He draws his sword from the scabbard at his side. He looks it over as if admiring the blade. Or just drawing out my torment, letting me have a good look at the weapon that is about to end my life.

He grasps the hilt with both hands and lifts it over his head, ready to strike down on my neck. That's when a blood-curdling screech of a war cry rings out and I can't quite believe my eyes. Aideen runs into view with that little dagger of hers in-hand. Feathers has just enough time to turn and look in confusion before she plunges the dagger deep into his right eye and up into his skull as she tackles him to the ground. The longsword clatters loudly as it hits the floor, abandoned.

I'm in shock. I blink rapidly and my strength is gone and I don't quite know what to do or how to react, if I even can at all. I close my eyes for a moment because I'm so drained. I feel a pressure against my wounded shoulder. And then I hear Aideen crying. Sob after sob after sob.

I force my eyes back open and turn my head to the right. She's bent over me, holding one of her blankets firmly against my shoulder and keening like someone has died. I'm not quite dead yet, Princess. Heh. I give her a very tired, warbling trill.

My lady gasps and looks over at me, tears all over her face. I smile weakly, but it's apparently enough to cause her entire face to light up.

She keeps pressure on my shoulder for what feels like a long time. Every now and then, she peels the blanket back to check my wound before covering it again. I can't quite tell how much time passes, but eventually she pulls the blanket off entirely. My wound must have clotted enough to be fine on its own, then. Good. I should be able to recover just fine with Aideen's help. She knows where the mountain stream is and we have buckets around here somewhere to carry water. If her jars of human food are inadequate, I suppose I could part with some gold coins from my hoard for her to go purchase some livestock to bring up from the village below.

The irony is not lost on me in this moment. Both Blue and Aideen's book indicated I'd likely die from her presence. Yet, even though her being here *did* place me in danger, the story did not play out as everyone says it does or should. The prince did not slay the dragon and retake the princess. Instead, the princess actually slayed the prince to retake the dragon.

I can't help but chortle at the thought, even though it causes a twinge of pain in my still-healing shoulder. Aideen looks over at me and I decide to do better by her, even though my voice is nothing but a croak at this point. "Aideen, *thank you*."

Loop

Written by

Estee Lee-Mountel

0530

Wake-up call. I startle into sudden wakefulness at my desk, scattering books and datapads. Trudge to the bathroom, splash some water on my face, and brush my teeth. Stayed up way too late last night studying for the promotion examinations but, dammit, I really want to make lieutenant. Commander Terjan keeps telling me that I'll do fine, that I'm more than ready. She had joked about sabotaging my exams so I'd stay on her team in Engineering because she'd hate to lose me after my promotion.

Someday, that's going to be me: someone people look up to and admire because I'm awesome and funny and damn good at my job. A good leader.

One step at a time. Focus.

Head down to the mess hall for breakfast. Scroll through messages on my personal device. Aw, Gav sent me a vid-message last night.

"Hey, sis. Don't stress yourself out, and I know you are. That's why I'm telling you: Don't. Stress. Out. You'll do fine and make your big brother proud. No matter what. Break's over. Gotta get back to my station. From my ship to yours, love ya. Gavin, out."

Save it. Put it in the "instant play" archive file. That's a good one to keep handy for the really bad days.

Ugh. What did they put in the oatmeal today? Oh well. Food is food. Better than starving.

"Beep. Beep. Beep."

There's my signal. No time to dawdle. Game face on.

0700

So far, it's been quiet. I spent the first hour of the shift doing the routine stuff we do every morning. Can't help but feel like something big is going to happen. Commander came in looking tense, like she's looking or waiting for something. I wonder what went on at the officers' meeting this morning. She's definitely worried about something.

Whatever it is, we'll be ready for it. I'm ready.

Or, maybe she had the oatmeal, too. My stomach hasn't been feeling that well, to be honest.

0830

Captain just left the deck; came down for a surprise inspection. Said they detected fluctuations from the engines' readouts to the bridge. I've been sitting here for the past hour and I haven't seen anything. I even pulled the panels out, opened her up, and everything. Nothing to report. If there was something to report, I'd have reported it. Really had to keep myself from blurting out, *Maybe you should have your watchstander checked.*

Those dumb ensigns think being assigned to the bridge means they're hot shit, just because they sit ten feet away from the captain. They're really not. Actually, they're just glorified couriers, if anything. Fuckers really get on my nerves sometimes.

Calm down. Refocus that energy.

Commander Terjan still looks worried about something. Maybe I should run a deeper diagnostic from my terminal. Just in case. I'd hate to let her down.

1006

Something's playing havoc with the sensors. Everything came back clean from the diagnostic but I'm beginning to see funny readings. I told Commander Terjan. She asked the bridge to see if they were seeing it too but, ironically, they hadn't noticed anything.

Things have been weird since we entered this sector. No one will tell us where we're going or what our mission is. Officers are suddenly secretive. Last night, everything seemed fine. A couple of the officers were in the lounge playing games and unwinding just like the rest of us. Business as usual.

What happened? I wonder if there's something environmental affecting everyone. Maybe I can rig up a scan from my terminal here and... There we go. There's got to be an answer to all of this.

Commander Terjan has gone from looking worried to just spaced out. Maybe she needs a little pick-me-up, like a snack and some coffee. I could sure use a refreshment, to be honest. It's hard to think on an empty stomach. I excuse myself, and my crewmates just glance at me with what looked like a cross between confusion and interest. The commander doesn't even acknowledge me.

What the hell is going on?

1227

Systems are going down ship-wide. Something happened when I went to go get my snack. Apparently, everyone on the ship decided to go for a snack, too. Everyone, except the officers. The officers have just been sitting there looking at nothing. They didn't even notice we were gone. Still, damn weird that all of us decided on a snack at the same time. Must be that fleet academy training. Guess none of us really outgrows that rigorous schedule at the academy.

Updated Commander Terjan on the problems I'd been able to fix and she... She's just sitting there. If she didn't blink from time to time, I'd think she was a statue or hologram or something. The chief medical officer seems to be the only one not affected by whatever's going on, though. I asked him to come down and look at Commander Terjan but the folks in the med lab tell me he's busy. When I asked them to contact him on his communicator, they only said that he just couldn't be reached right now, except by the PA system. And we were told to stay off the PA system unless it was something that affected the whole ship.

I can feel a pulse. I can hear her breathing. Aside from that, though, it's like... The lights are on, but no one's home.

I guess I'll keep holding out until he has a chance to come down to engineering and see the commander. No time to worry about that now. I need to make sure I'm doing everything I can from my end or none of this will matter. Other people from the ship are reporting in, so at least there's that. Even if the officers aren't responding or doing anything, at least we can keep the ship running until we figure all of this out.

If we can figure this out, that is.

That's not positive thinking. What did the manual say about keeping cool in a crisis situation?

Not important. Got to focus.

Shit, not another damn alert. What is it this time?

1312

Reports from other parts of the ship aren't good. Navigation just told us we're locked in on a collision course with a massive brown dwarf. There's nothing they can do about it. They said it's lucky they were able to find out this much by tearing into the terminals and forcing the system to tell them. The science and medical labs said they couldn't detect anything in the environment that could be causing this weird behavior amongst the officers. And, since the snack time incident, there hasn't been another case of the entire crew seemingly operating on a subliminal signal from a hive mind.

Wait a second. Where's the report from the environmental diagnostic I was running a few hours back?

Scanning, scanning... Computer said it finished and compiled the data more than an hour ago. And then it deleted the results immediately. Who ordered the results to be deleted?! No one? How can that be? Someone has to give the order before the computer can take action. Is it the commander? No, she hasn't moved. She barely looks conscious. And Lithor's been keeping an eye on the commander the whole time; she's got the sharpest eyes out of all of us and, if the commander's even so much as twitched, Lithor would have seen it.

Then someone else ordered the results deleted. Who would have that authority? Someone on the bridge.

Engineering to bridge.

"Bridge, here."

Have any of the officers up there done anything?

"Not a thing. We have eyes on them, just to make sure and they haven't even moved a pinky. If I didn't know any better, I'd say they're all asleep with their eyes open. Why do you ask?"

I ran an environmental diagnostic on a lark, just to see what I could see. Someone or something had the results deleted immediately after they were finished and compiled.

"What?! That can't happen without authorization from an officer."

Yeah, I know. That's what I'm trying to figure out.

"I'm guessing you already ruled out the chief engineer?"

We've been keeping an eye on Commander Terjan. She hasn't moved.

"I was afraid you'd say that. We'll get it figured out. If we find a way to keep from crashing into this brown dwarf, that is."

I hear ya. We'll keep working on a solution. Engineering, out.

Check with science and medical. No, their officers haven't moved, either. Chief medical officer's been running around with a crew of assistants and nurses, nowhere near a terminal that could access the results or systems, for that matter. Technically, those results could have been deleted by any high-ranking crewman on this ship from any systems terminal.

... From any systems terminal.

Engineering to bridge!

"Bridge, here. Did you find out who deleted your results?"

No, but I have an idea. Anyone can access data from any systems terminal, right?

"Uh, yeah, but how does that help us?"

So, if you're locked out of navigation, maybe I can bypass the controls from here by diverting power and systems to my terminal in engineering!

"Holy shit. That's brilliant!"

Stand by. And keep your fingers crossed.

"You got it, engineering."

Okay, first things first. Set firewalls and protections on this terminal. Isolate Navigation from the rest of the ship systems. Shut down Navigation systems and reboot. Reroute power from Navigation to Engineering. Bring up Navigation on my terminal. Accessing... Accessing... Access granted! Set new coordinates and vectors. Wait, what? Something's shutting me out of Navigation. The system is rebooting to reroute power back to the main Navigation computer. It's isolating *me* and shutting *me* out of the system!

Maybe one more try? No, I'm restricted to energy readouts on the engines. I can't even look at the other subsystems in engineering.

"Engineering?"

Sorry, bridge. It didn't work. It looked like... I can't believe it. Did that really happen? *It looked like the system was actively working against me and trying to outsmart me. Like it figured out what I was doing and outmaneuvered me.*

"Damn. Good try, though. Seriously, it was a good effort."

Thanks. Engineering, out.

1534

Bridge crew just updated the rest of the ship on our situation. We're about two hours out from impact with the brown dwarf. I can feel the inertial dampeners working against the weather coming off of the massive thing already. There's obviously a bug in the system and it wants us, or at least this ship, dead. Diagnostics won't do us much good because the system will likely either tailor the results or just get rid of the—

That's what happened to my results from environmental diagnostic. The system deleted it. It didn't want me or anyone knowing what was going on, or what it was doing. The answer's so obvious! Why didn't I see it before?

Hell, it probably used the credentials of any of the officers stored in the data caches to do the job, and then covered its tracks.

So, if I can't go about solving this the conventional way since the system is against me, what are the unconventional ways, then?

I'll bring the fight to them. What I can't do virtually, I'll have to do physically.

Toolkits, spanners, screwdrivers, wire strippers. Pry open the panel to my terminal, and start tearing into the guts of the machine. Wires in my way, clip snip clip. Take this circuit board out of its holding, switch it with this one. Connect that wire with this node here. Plug the adapter from this hub to the one over there. The screen's rebooting. Good. It's a hell of a lot better than the faked energy readings it was feeding me earlier. We're getting somewhere!

What the--?

Vanny? Lithor? *Commander?!*

What are you guys doing? Let me go! I think I'm onto something!

"We know."

They're talking in unison. That's not academy training taking over, anymore. But, kicking them and running like hell is. The ship shakes, shudders, bucking suddenly to the right. Helps me shake off my crewmates and run out of engineering. I stumble through right as the doors slide shut. The ship knows I'm trying to escape, trying to stop whatever it is that it wants to accomplish.

I can hear footsteps coming for me from both directions. Shit. Where can I...?

Nowhere to run.

The red alert alarms start sounding all over the ship. Were they always this loud or does it just seem that way because I can't escape whatever's going to happen? The terrifying noise of impending doom, like in the flashy feature vids: your heart beating so hard and so fast that your veins are wide open, inundated, and all you can hear is your rushing blood. Your vision starts to go red from all of it.

Maybe that's why it's called "red alert."

Here they come.

At least I tried. Really, I did, Gav. I'll tell Mom and Dad hi for you.

0530

Wake-up call.

Was that...? Was all of that just...? Man, that must have been a terrible dream. Just a bad dream. I think I've been studying too much. Too many late nights, too many stim packs. Bleary, confused, I pick up my books and datapads, then head to the bathroom. Splash some water on my face, brush my teeth. Wish I could shake off the feelings from that dream. It felt so real. Too real, honestly.

I think I'll make sure I get a decent, full night's sleep tonight once I'm off duty.

Besides, I don't think Commander Terjan was serious in her threats about sabotaging my efforts to ace the exam. She says she'd hate to see me go and wants me to stay on her team. It's funny, really. When she says stuff like that, I actually believe it, that I'm actually that good as an engineer and tech. That's how I'd like to be someday: a leader who can inspire her crew just by saying a few words, but still be laid back and feel like one of the little guys.

I can't get distracted. Everything will happen in due time.

No wonder I'm having nightmares.

Food solves everything, though. Get down to the mess hall; still early and not a lot of people are up and about yet. Scrolling through messages on my personal device while I eat. Huh, it's a vid-message from Gavin.

"Hey, sis. Don't stress yourself out, and I know you are. That's why I'm telling you: Don't. Stress. Out. You'll do fine and make your big brother proud. No matter what. Break's over. Gotta get back to my station. From my ship to yours, love ya. Gavin, out."

That's weird. I could have sworn that was the same message I got from Gavin in my dream last night. Maybe I heard it in my sleep as it was recording. This is what I get for having an older model instead of upgrading like everyone else.

"What's happening?"

"That's not supposed to happen."

What was that? I think someone left the mic to the PA system on by accident. Hopefully they don't say anything embarrassing. The fleet would never let them live it down.

Man, this oatmeal tastes terrible. On second thought, I'm not that hungry anymore. Guess I can always start my shift early.

0745

Commander Terjan looks worried. Something must have happened at the morning briefing.

I'm getting this weird sense of déjà vu. Didn't this happen in last night's dream, too?

You know, just to be safe, I'm going to re-run the routine stuff I did already. I'd hate for the commander to be in trouble because of something one of us did.

Whoa, the captain's down here? What's going on that she couldn't ask us over the intercom?

"Commander, we've been getting strange readings from the engines and several of the engineering subsystems up on the bridge. Can you confirm?"

"Ma'am? Everything's been quiet down here. No one's reported so much as a wayward ion."

Everyone's staring at me like I have the answers. They actually want my opinion on the matter? *All routine scans came back clean, captain. We've been monitoring everything and nothing's out of place. No fluctuations, no funny readings. Nothing.*

I'll tell you what, though: those damned watchstanders on the bridge think they're so damn important just because they get to be on the bridge with you, captain! Think it, don't feel it. I really hope it isn't written all over my face. Oh, please, don't let it show.

"Something must be causing those readings, however. Commander Terjan, I want you and your team to do a full scan and diagnostic. I don't care if you have to open up the damn terminals to do it. I'd rather be safe and assured."

"Aye aye, ma'am. You heard her, people. Let's get to work. We'll report to you as soon as we're finished, captain."

"No, I'd rather stay here, actually. If I can help in some way, let me know."

"Sure thing, captain. Come on. Hop to it!"

I'm all about showing respect for the chain of command, but I have never seen Commander Terjan grovel. She's not the groveling sort. There's something awfully strange about the captain, too. I just wish I could put my finger on it. No one else seems bothered by it. Or, more accurately, no one's daring to show it.

I better focus. I hate feeling like I'm being watched. I hate it even more now with the captain and commander both acting so damn weird. Come to think of it, it feels like all of the officers have been acting strange. Seems like it started when we entered this sector. Pretty sure everyone and everything were fine before we entered our night cycle— before we transited to this place, wherever we are.

Okay, now I know something's not right. That's just too weird to be coincidence that stuff from my dream last night keep happening in real time. Is whatever's affecting the officers getting to me--?

"It's happening again."

"Try scanning ahead."

Did you find something, Lithor? Vanny?

Vanny and Lithor are both giving me blank expressions. They exchange glances before Lithor finally answers. "Uh, what?"

I thought I heard one of you say that something was happening again and to try scanning ahead.

They look at each other. Then they look at the commander and captain in turns, both of whom are acting like the conversation isn't happening. Vanny gets up, wipes his hands on his uniform, and shakes his head. "Neither of us said a thing. Maybe you're hearing things— probably because you stayed up too late studying last night and stressing so much."

"It can't do that. It's not supposed to be doing that!"

I'm looking straight at Vanny and Lithor, and that definitely didn't come from either of them. Maybe it's the person who left their mic on for the PA system?

Did you guys hear—

1227

Systems are going down ship-wide. Something happened when I went to go get my snack. Apparently, everyone on the ship decided to go for a snack, too. Everyone, except the officers. The officers have just been sitting there looking at nothing. They didn't even notice we were gone. Still, damn weird that all of us decided on a snack at the same time. Must be that fleet academy training.

I... I don't remember getting that snack. Actually, come to think of it, I don't remember the last few hours at all. Maybe Vanny and Lithor are right. All of the pressure I've been putting on myself isn't healthy. I need to relax a little bit. Wish I could figure out how. I know the doc's busy and all with the officers acting weird, but maybe he can see me for a second. I can't be blacking out, especially with the ship in crisis.

I need to help find out what's going on.

Hey, Vanny? Lithor? I'm heading up to see the doctor real quick.

They just nod absently. They're working hard to solve this mystery, too.

I head up to the medical and science decks, and everyone is in a big hurry. They're probably busier than anyone else on the ship, trying to see what's wrong with the officers, in addition to helping the rest of the crew figure out why our ship's acting the way it is. The chief medical officer's nowhere to be found, though. I grab one of the aides and ask him where his commander is, but he can't tell me.

There's too much work to be done to waste time tracking down the doctor. Maybe whatever's happening to me will go away if I just keep my mind off of it.

1312

Reports from other parts of the ship aren't good. Navigation just told us we're locked in on a collision course with a massive brown dwarf. There's nothing they can do about it. They said it's lucky they were able to find out this much by tearing into the terminals and forcing the system to tell them. The science and medical labs said they couldn't detect anything in the environment that could be causing this weird behavior amongst the officers.

I think I remember ordering the computer to run my own tests for anomalies in the environment, but I can't seem to find the results anywhere. I don't remember asking for the test, but I can't be sure. Not anymore. There's just too much going on. Too much strangeness. Hearing things. Missing hours of the day at a time.

I can't be sure.

My terminal's telling me that I asked for a full spectrum analysis of the ship's environment hours ago after the captain left Engineering, but there are no results. Archives say that they were deleted immediately after. Something's going on and, whoever or whatever is causing all of this, doesn't want me to know about it.

I wish I could say that whatever's happening isn't affecting me but... I can't be sure. I'm just not sure.

Come on. Focus. The results from the environmental scan. There's something important about it. Not the results themselves, but I just know they're pointing to something bigger. This happened in my dream last night, too. That's how I know it's important.

I'm starting to think last night's dream wasn't just a dream.

"It's starting to fray and unravel already."

"We were lucky to find this one in the first place, you know."

"Yeah, but how reliable is it? Look at what's happening!"

Who the hell is saying that?! *Lithor? Vanny?*

I look around for my crewmates, but they're nowhere to be found. Wait, no. They're here, but they've become living statues like Commander Terjan. But, that also means the conversation I just heard came out of nowhere. Again. Okay, take a breath and think rationally. This isn't science fiction. What could be causing audio anomalies?

Think: Whatever's affecting the ship's systems might be sending feedback through the intercoms. Or maybe there's someone else on the ship who's still sane— or, at least, unaffected by the thing that's rendered most of the crew ineffective. I like that hypothesis a hell of a lot more than the possibility of hearing voices from nowhere.

Now that I've put that to rest for the moment, I need to figure out how to keep the ship from crashing into the brown dwarf. Hey, if Navigation can't access the ship's systems, what's stopping me? Maybe I can try to get into the nav computer's programming and redirect us to some place less lethal.

Okay, first things first. Set firewalls and protections on this terminal. Isolate Navigation from the rest of the ship systems. Shut down Navigation systems and reboot. (This happened in my dream, too, didn't it? No, stay focused.) Reroute power from Navigation to Engineering. Bring up Navigation on my terminal. Accessing... Accessing... Access granted! Set new coordinates and vectors. (This definitely happened. I know it. I can feel it.) Wait, what? Something's shutting me out of Navigation. The system is rebooting to reroute power back to the main Navigation computer. It's isolating *me* and shutting *me* out of the system!

Dammit! Now I've just got these stupid faked energy readings from the engine room. Wait, Navigation said they had to literally tear into their terminals to force the system to tell them what was going on.

That's what I'm going to have to do, too, then.

Not here, though. I can't risk having my crewmates see what I'm doing, even if they're barely conscious. I slip the nearby tools into my pockets and get up, stretching and yawning for effect.

I'm just going to go for a drink. I need to take a break.

Oh, that was smooth. Very convincing. They might put you in the running for a major award. Good thing the audience is practically comatose or they'd start throwing rotting tomatoes at you, like in those old-timey films from 20th century Earth.

I just need to find a terminal that's discreet and out of the way. Actually, one of the service tunnels might be best. I definitely wouldn't have to worry about someone finding me in an access hatch.

"What are you doing away from your post, ensign?"

Normally, the captain asking me such a routine question wouldn't make me jump, even if she just came up behind me out of the blue. But, the entire crew is here with her, and they all just asked the question at the same time.

I'm just stretching my legs, ma'am. I needed a break, that's all.

"We find that to be highly unlikely."

This can't end well.

0530

Wake-up call.

I'm not falling for this again. I know what's going on now. Can't fool me this time. And this time, it won't take me hours to figure this all out. Because this time... This time, I remember everything from the last go-around.

Wash my face, brush my teeth. Nothing out of the ordinary yet. Look at my personal device as I head out of my quarters, and there's the message from Gavin again. Wish I could see him, if for no other reason than to say good-bye or, at least, that I love him. No time for that mushy stuff, though. There's work to be done.

"I told you not to stress, sis."

Gav? What the hell are you doing here?! You're supposed to be across the galaxy.

"What, and abandon my sister when she needs me the most? Not likely."

How did you get here?

"That's not important right now. Come on. Focus. Are you getting breakfast?"

No, I was hoping to skip the terrible oatmeal this time. I've already had it twice in a row.

"Bad idea. You need to give things time to happen before you can act. Get breakfast."

But I don't want to! Seriously, the oatmeal was disgusting!

"Now you're just whining. Get something other than the oatmeal, dummy. See? Problem solved."

Okay, okay. You win.

I turn around to get to the Mess Hall, but I'm all alone in the hallway again. Gavin was just here! Where did he go?! He was here, wasn't he?

"Things are beginning to manifest! Fascinating!"

"'Fascinating'?! That's all you can say?"

"No one's ever encountered this phenomenon before! This is quite exciting."

"Just shut up and move ahead."

Those voices again. They didn't start up this early last time. I wonder what they really are.

"Did you see that?!"

Wait, see what? What am I supposed to to—

0800

Commander Terjan looks worried. Captain's here for the surprise inspection, citing the weird readings from Engineering that they got on the bridge. And here I am, up to my elbows with wires and circuit boards, the very guts of the terminal at my station. I'm starting to wonder what happens to me before I go back to my 0530 wake-up call. All I remember is that things look dire— a situation I can't escape. Do I die? Am I torn apart by my shipmates— the same way I'm tearing apart my terminal?

"Something bothering you, ensign?"

No, captain. Just making sure I got this wire back into its node here. I like to be thorough in my work, ma'am.

"I like that sort of attention to detail in my crew. Keep it up."

That was a little too close. I need to keep focused, or at least stop spacing out. I'll get an opening here soon. Hell, I'll even make sure to run that deep-scan diagnostic after I'm done putting my terminal back together.

1033

The commander went from looking worried to blank, which means it's probably snack time. Now's my chance to get out of the Engineering decks without causing too much suspicion. That's the idea, anyway.

I start making my way to the small lounge one deck up. No one's tried to stop me yet, so that's the good news. If this is anything like the last go-around, everyone except for the officers will be getting up for a snack, too, and that should keep them distracted. In fact, now that I'm looking around, the halls are completely empty.

"Should we stop this?"

"Let's just see what happens. We might actually get the answers we need."

Those damn voices again. I know it's wishful thinking, but I hope it's someone else on the ship trying to do the same thing I am: figure out what's causing all of this, and not get caught in the meantime.

"Ensign? What are you doing away from your post? Aren't you going down to the lounge?"

Turn slowly. Carefully. *Doc? I thought you were busy treating the officers.*

"You haven't answered my question, ensign."

What, about going to the lounge? I had been going in that direction, but I realized I'm not all that hungry. I think the oatmeal from this morning has upset my stomach.

"Thank God! I was afraid I was the only one on the ship who hasn't gone completely mad!"

What do you mean, sir?

"Between everyone else on the ship suddenly getting a case of the munchies and the lethargic officers, the prognosis looked pretty grim."

Why aren't you all spaced out like the other officers?

He shrugs. "I don't know. I was finishing up some lab reports from the previous mission when reports started coming in about erratic behavior and then the sudden lethargy in all officers, even the captain. Before I could do anything about the officers, everyone else left for a snack."

Wait, you didn't go to this morning's briefing?

"No, I had too much work to do. I turned off my badge communicator and practically all forms of contact except the emergency line to my office. Hell, I probably missed the call to go to the meeting."

Doc's eyes widen as the answer dawns on him, too. "That explains me. What about you?"

Now there's the million-credit question. I don't think telling the chief medical officer that I've been essentially living the same day over and over again while hearing voices and hallucinating about my brother is a good idea, however. Not when I just convinced him I'm the only other sane person on the ship.

I'm not entirely sure, sir. I have a hunch, however, that whatever answers we're looking for are hidden deep within the ship's systems.

"Commander Terjan tells me you're one of her best down in Engineering, and I agree with your assessment. Whatever's happening isn't medical, that's for sure. I'll leave this to you. What do you propose?"

Since we can't trust any of the ship's readouts from the terminals, I can hook up my personal device into the ship's computers through an access panel tucked away in the maintenance shafts.

"You're going to hack into the ship?"

I wince. *You could say that, sir.*

"It's as good a plan as any. Better than running around the ship and hiding from the rest of the crew. Lead on."

You're coming with me?

He pauses, thinking. He doesn't like it, but he says, "You're right. They're likely looking for me, as I'm the only officer unaffected and unaccounted for, and I'd only slow you down. Get to the bottom of this, ensign."

Aye aye, sir.

We move off in different directions. I start making random turns, using maintenance ladders to go from deck to deck. I don't know how good it— whatever *it* is affecting my shipmates— is at tracking people, but it wouldn't hurt to be careful. Finally, I open up a panel in the wall and duck into the maintenance shaft. I seal the panel again, making sure it looks undisturbed.

Then, I start crawling deeper into the ship, where I hope I'm less likely to get caught.

A few wires here, a node there, fashion a port out of this spare part and a piece of the paneling, plug that into the device, and I'm in. That was the easy part. I convince the system to show me the ship's background logs from last night. There's the usual boring stuff, but the data seems to become garbled after it registers entering the new sector. A lot of junk data, entries that make no sense. Extensive corruption. That explains why the ship's gone haywire, but it doesn't explain how the computers got so corrupted, nor does it explain the crew.

Wait, there's an event buried in the middle of a bunch of gibberish. Timestamp puts it right as we entered the sector. An anomaly detected, then dismissed because it was miniscule and fleeting. Without additional knowledge, anyone would think it was just space weather.

Computer, widen parameters for anomalies to include data streams and energy used to transfer information throughout the ship.

"Analyzing."

I sit back while my little device puts all of its processing power to work. Oh, if only Gavin could see me now— hacking into the ship's systems, of all things! I guess they can always court martial me after everything's over. If I survive, that is.

"That sort of thinking will get you nowhere, sis."

And, just like that, my big brother is suddenly sitting in the maintenance shaft with me.

Gav? Please tell me you're not just a hallucination.

"I'm not just a hallucination. Sort of."

That doesn't help.

"Look, that's not important. You're doing the best you can. And you've almost got this figured out. That, right there, is the important bit."

I know. I still can't help but feel like this is all for nothing.

"Not quite. Don't let that get to you, though. Just focus."

My device suddenly chirps. "Analysis complete."

I grab my device, watching the results scroll by. I look up again as the information compiles, and Gavin's gone. I had expected as much, but I was really hoping I wouldn't have to face this alone.

And there it is: it looks like junk data attached to every single byte and packet that's been sent throughout the ship for the last several hours. There's been more than enough time to multiply, to dominate the systems and the ship's central computing servers.

The same servers that allow crew to communicate with one another using their built-in badge communicators. The same ones that once passively monitored vitals as we sleep in our shipboard cots. And the same servers that house the ship's core information like chain of command, roster, and manifest.

"I had too much work to do. I turned off my badge communicator..."

My hand immediately goes to my left breast, and all I feel is fabric. In my sleep-deprived stupor, I had completely forgotten to put on my badge when I changed into a fresh uniform.

"YOU FOUND US."

The tinny sound of the synthesized voice is deafening within the confines of the maintenance shaft, like someone turned up the volume for the PA system to maximum. I can feel the speakers in the panels straining with the sheer amount of sound being pumped out of them. At this point, though, I've got nothing left to lose, no more logical choices or solutions.

Why? I'm screaming out the words, my throat raw and stinging with the effort. *Why do this? Why this ship?*

"YOU ATTACKED US FIRST."

We didn't do anything! We just entered the sector and did nothing else.

"THIS IS OUR SECTOR. YOU INVADED US. YOU ATTACKED US."

With just our passing by, you thought we were invaders. Why didn't you try to communicate with us, or at least let us explain?

"NO EXPLANATIONS. DIRECTIVE CLEAR."

It's intelligent. It's sentient. It's pure energy, and it's living. And it's doing what any intelligent, sentient creature would do when it thinks it's being attacked: defend itself. I slump against the panel, ignoring the flood of code and gibberish that has taken over my device. Strangely, calmly, I begin to marvel at what I've found. The sophistication is so beyond me, and all I can do is be in awe of it. It even figured out our physiology and exploited something as simple as the electric currents that send information between neurons and nerves and the brain. Amazing.

Something's not quite right, though. *If you infiltrated our ship's systems, then you must know what our primary mission is. You know that we're a peaceful vessel!*

"YOU HAVE POWERFUL WEAPONS ON THIS SHIP. YOU ARE NOT PEACEFUL. YOU ARE ARMED. YOU ARE INVADERS."

"Ensign? Have you discovered anything?"

I jump. To my relief, it's only Doc.

Doc! How did you find me?

"I evaded my pursuers and had a hunch you'd be down here." He shifts and I catch sight of a metallic glint on his uniform. The tiny light of the badge's transmitter blinks steadily.

My relief shrivels up. I meet the chief medical officer's eyes and see a brief flash of humanity, mournful and almost apologetic. My device sparks and pops and dies. The irony isn't lost on me.

The same thing is probably happening to this recording right now.

Oh, I know what's going on now. It explains the déjà vu and my big brother suddenly popping up when I'm stressing out, among other things. I can hear the approach of my crewmates converging on my location, their unwieldy bodies careening and crashing through the maintenance shafts as they're guided by tiny alien puppeteers. The chief medical officer has one of my shoulders pinned against the access panel to prevent my escape— as if I actually had somewhere to run to. With my free hand, I feel the little bump near the base of my skull where the fleet's medical staff had inserted the standard issue recording chip upon my assignment to this ship: my biosynthetic black box.

I don't even know what's worse: realizing that I'm supposed to be dead, or realizing that I'm actually stuck in this recording. That I *am* a recording, like it's some sort of technological purgatory for poor, unwitting souls like me.

"It's losing integrity fast."

"It was actually thinking— conscious and sentient. It... *She* knows what's happening! She's self-aware!"

Those damn voices again. Whatever or whoever they are, I hope they learn a little compassion. Maybe an utter lack of compassion is how you get assigned to a desk job at Fleet HQ.

"With this evidence, though, we can make sure this never happens again. We've been losing ships for months, and now we know why. I'll send the report to Fleet Command so they can quarantine the sector."

"Wish we could run it one more time."

"Do you realize what else we've discovered here?! This isn't some mere recording anymore! Even the contents of the 'recording' altered and shifted as she figured things out. Let her go to her rest. She deserves that at the very least. She's finished her mission."

"Oh please. Don't get sentimental on me now. Just cut the power and kill it."

End loop.

Gatri's Diner

Written by

Estee Lee-Mountel

R*ing-a-ling-a-ling!*

"Welcome to Gatri's Diner. What can I get ya?"

"Just a platter of the breakfast special and a mug of your strongest. No cream."

"Rough day, huh?"

"Yeah, had a deadline to meet for some big spender. The boss didn't want to let 'em down. Speaking of bosses, where's the Cap?"

"Busy. You know how it is."

"Captain" Gatri Vox smiled as she listened to the exchange, hidden behind a fortress of sanitizer, pancake mix, and noise. Oh, that wonderful noise: meat on the griddle; silverware against dishes; cups and glasses set upon the counter; utensils meeting cookware; and, best of all, the conversations. She once called it the song of the universe, voices from a myriad of sentient species coming together in mosaic harmony.

Here, stationed on one of the sector's busiest shipping lanes between several large mining operations, the Cap'n and her crew saw everything the galaxy has to offer, and then some. Big or small, they all come to Gatri's for one thing: a nice, hot meal.

It's an unspoken, unnamed yearning in every sentient creature's heart. After hours of toiling, working, meeting deadlines, and being nothing more than a serial number and tool, there's a distinct hunger gnawing at the mind. It's the silent cry to be recognized as a living, breathing person— a person with ideas, wants, dreams, hopes, and regrets. The hunger can be quelled, buried under the trappings of duty and responsibility, but never sated until it's been properly fed. Even in this advanced age of space travel and technology, while philosophers ponder and scientists theorize, no one can quite explain the apparently magical properties of a well-cooked meal.

Gatri cleared off a table, nodding in farewell to the group of gas rig engineers coming off from a 10-hour shift. After eating their fill here, they'll head back to their on-site living quarters for several hours of shut-eye before returning to work again.

The airlock slammed open and then shut again, making the bell at the door ring wildly. Everyone fell silent, turning to stare at the wild-eyed newcomer who refused to meet anyone's gaze, shifting from foot to foot. As one, everyone now turned to stare at Gatri.

Because, when in doubt, look to the captain for the answers.

She moved carefully, casually. Her voice was pitched low. "Welcome to my diner. Have a seat, and tell me what can I get for you."

"Get? What? Oh, right. Yeah. Uh, I don't know. Maybe..."

"Maybe we can start with some eggs and toast. See how you feel after that."

"Eggs. Toast. Yeah."

Gatri navigated the newcomer to a seat at the counter. He hunched in his seat, long fingers drumming on the countertop. Before she could get to the kitchen, the airlock slammed open and shut once more. The bell chimed for more than three minutes.

"Nobody move," a deep, used-to-bossing-people-around voice said behind her. "Sector Patrol. We're looking for someone."

Gatri turned. There, at the entrance, were two Sector Patrol officers, trying to look in command and very important. They quailed under her gaze.

"Welcome to my diner, you two. Pick a table, and tell me what I can get started for you."

"We're not here for a heart attack on a plate! We're looking for—"

"There!" the second officer cut in, his voice cracking with excitement. "There he is! We got 'im!"

The officers moved toward the anxious newcomer, who had since tried to hide behind his jacket's meager collar and cover his face with an arm. Gatri stepped into the officers' path.

"It's against house rules to bother other customers," she said, as if they were discussing nothing more than the traffic. "Now, sit down and eat your breakfast like good officers."

The two officers exchanged baffled looks. "Wait, breakfast? We didn't order..."

"How long have you been on this case?"

"Uh, the last six or seven hours?"

"Nah, it's definitely been at least ten," the first officer said as she shook her head.

"Right. So, when was the last time either of you ate something?"

"Well, we picked up some snacks..."

"An actual meal that you sat down and ate like proper folks?"

Silence.

"That's what I thought. Now," Gatri said, gesturing to the chairs on either side of the mystified newcomer, "sit."

The newcomer stared at her, wide-eyed. She only nodded, a friendly inclination of her head, as she headed toward the kitchen. "Scramble me some eggs with a couple of interceptors, plus two full haulers."

"Aye, Cap'n!" came the reply from the kitchen. Satisfied, Gatri turned back to her customers and leaned against the counter. They sat still, not daring to move under her critical gaze. Around them, the rest of the diner resumed its usual business. The situation was in the captain's hands. Everyone else could relax.

"Mind telling me why you all came barging into my diner this morning?" Gatri said.

The two officers started speaking at the same time, while the still unnamed newcomer groaned and glared at the officers in turn. Gatri barked a sharp order and they lapsed into hurried silence. She nodded to the newcomer, then fixed the officers with a piercing look, daring them to speak. They didn't.

"You came here first, so you may as well start the tale."

"Uh, well, I guess, um..."

"Why don't you start with your name, son."

The newcomer lifted his head and looked Gatri in the eyes for the first time, though he remained huddled in his seat. "Zaxon, ma'am. But everyone just calls me Zax, if you please."

"Alright, Zax. What brings you to my diner this morning?"

"I'm an engineer on one of those big freighters the mining companies use to haul each shipment. We'd just docked with the facility over by that gas giant, Panthok Seven, and I was going through my routine stuff— you know, checking the lines, making sure all of the valves were adjusted and set just right. Then these two come banging through the engineering deck, ruining ALL of my work..."

"Hey!" the first officer interjected, jabbing an angry finger at Zax. "If you hadn't broken Intergalactic Law Statute four five zero four seven dash two... OW!"

Gatri smacked the officer's offending digit with a cleaning rag. "It's not polite to point. Or interrupt."

The officer sullenly nursed her hurt finger. "You're not very nice, you know that?"

"'Nice' isn't what keeps me in business." She reached behind her and set the plates down onto the counter without looking. "Hush, now. Eat up. I'll be back in a few minutes. And, no fighting."

Unwilling to incur the wrath of the captain, the trio set into their food with a large side of thick-cut, awkward silence. Satisfied, Gatri grabbed another tray of food and headed off to serve other tables. She stopped to chat with some merchants on their way to a trader's convention near the capital worlds. Apparently, business was good thanks to the addition of new hyperspace lanes— which also meant cheaper supplies and less haggling on Gatri's part.

The first time Gatri passed Zax and the officers, they were still eating with stiff, mechanical movements. She only gave them a cursory glance as she showed a group of mineral miners from Panthok Prime to their table. Sure, it wasn't progress, but at least neither officers nor engineer had threatened violence at one another in her absence.

On her second flyby, laden with a tray of fifteen vegetable-based omelets for Table 27's band of traveling ascetic monks, she heard Zax ask for the ketchup. His request was met with a silent, curt gesture that gave him his requested condiment and nothing else. After she finished checking on the status of Table 33's meals, she noticed that Zax had huddled even further into his seat in the stony silence. The captain closed her eyes for only a moment, telling herself to be patient, to allow them the time they needed.

It wasn't until Gatri closed out the bill for a couple of methane-breathing tourists and said farewell to the mineral miners when something finally happened. She heard the clatter of a butter knife falling onto the floor, followed by the usual— and quite necessary— swearing. Before she or any of the waitstaff could move to intervene, the second officer offered his unused knife to Zax.

"Here. I wasn't using it anyway," he said.

"Oh, thanks..." Zax said, trailing off, unsure.

"Name's Arnett," the second officer said as Zax took the knife to apply butter to his toast.

"Well, thanks, Officer Arnett."

"Nah, just Arnett. Hell, you can call me Arnie."

On the other side of Zax, the first officer pushed her empty plate back with a satisfied sigh. "It's better than most of the nicknames the others give him," she said, laughing.

Arnie rolled his eyes good-naturedly. "And that's Tana, my partner. Unfortunately."

Tana waved, grinning wolfishly. "Unfortunately for me, you mean."

Gatri returned to clear the dishes away. "Sounds like you folks had a good meal."

"Yes, ma'am," Zax said. "Thank you."

"Now, will you three tell me what's going on?"

They exchanged glances with one another. Zax and Arnie looked at Tana, who gave a resigned shrug.

"Arnie and I got a lead on this smuggling ring we've been working to bust. We talked to the informant, who led us to another lead, and another until we ended up with a ship name and the smuggled cargo to look out for."

"That brought them to the ship I was working on," Zax continued. "Except, I'm no smuggler. I'm just a grease monkey, some no-name engineer."

"When we came aboard," Arnie said, "the captain gave us the go-ahead to investigate the ship. We found Zax here in engineering, hiding a specimen from the smuggling shipment. He ran and we chased him here."

Gatri turned her attention back to Zax. Despite the relaxed and decidedly less hostile environment, he was still huddled into his chair.

"Give it up, son."

Slowly, carefully, Zax sat up and opened his jacket. Nestled in the crook of his arm was a small mammal with long, floppy ears, a moist nose, ridiculously huge eyes, and a fluffy tail. It looked up at Gatri and emitted a small sound like a soft *wheek* before tucking its nose back into its paws.

"I found the little guy running around engineering, scared for its life," Zax said. "I'd just caught it when Tana and Arnie showed up. They thought I was the smuggler, trying to secure my cargo so I'd get paid by whoever wants this poor thing." He paused, looking thoughtfully at the tiny creature in his arms. "I just wanted to make sure it would be safe."

"If you're not the smuggler, Zax," Tana said, "then there's someone on your crew who is. Can you think of anyone who might be the real bad guy?"

"Anything you've heard or seen could be helpful," Arnie said.

Zaxon paused, thinking hard, then nodded. "There was a guy in navigation who would usually be the first one off the ship for shore leave or anything else. If the ship was docked, he'd be gone. But he'd been sticking around the last couple of ports."

"Got anything else that seemed off to you?" Tana said. "We need a little more to go on here."

"Yeah, he came to visit engineering a couple of times." Zax's eyes widened. The words came quick now, spurred on by his excitement. "When we first met, he told me he hated the engineering deck because he couldn't stand the smell."

Arnie clapped Zax on the shoulder in elation, nearly knocking the poor creature out of the other man's arms. "That's our guy!"

The three of them jumped up and bolted for the airlock, then stopped. Tana fished around in her pockets for her wallet. Gatri held up her hand and waved them on.

"It's on the house. Get going before that guy skips port."

There was a jumbled chorus of thanks, punctuated by the wild, excited jingling of the bell at the airlock. A few heads looked up, then went back to their meals. Gatri turned to heave the cart of dirty dishes into the back. Behind her, she heard the airlock open with a smooth swoosh to admit another shift of hungry and tired shipyard workers. The dishes could wait.

She wiped her hands on a nearby sanicloth and snatched up some menus as she swept out of the kitchen.

"Welcome to Gatri's Diner, folks. What can I get ya?"

Worlds Collide

Written by

Millie Jean Warren

Contributions by

Estee Lee-Mountel

“This world is strange.”

A voice floated through the void on solar winds. It had a youthful lilt, which undermined its attempts to come across as calm, mysterious, and wise. “It’s complete with beings who hold an abundance of knowledge, and yet, their ignorance somehow manages to soar.”

The voice’s seemingly older and presumptuously wiser counterpart didn’t hesitate, of course, to poke at the younger’s obvious pretenses. “Even we Gods do not understand everything.”

An awkward, seething pause. “Quit it.” The former pushed aside its irritation at being interrupted and continued. “What these beings have yet to learn is that there is an intricate web that connects multiple dimensions together. Multiple worlds existing at once—”

“Remember,” the latter interrupted yet again, “you’re talking to humans. You don’t want to confuse them.”

“Thanks for the tip, but this isn’t my first time talking to humans.”

"There is a reason why they're having you practice this now, you know."

"What do you mean?"

"Remember last time?"

There was another long pause as the intelligence behind the first voice thought hard. "What are you talking about? I did just fine!"

"Oh, yes, you're absolutely right."

"So then, I'll just continue." It stopped, suddenly self-conscious and unsure. "I mean, unless you have some sort of feedback for me."

"No, no," the elder one said airily. "Please. Do continue. You're doing *such* a lovely job."

The first voice gave a small cough, buying time. "Ah, m-multiple worlds existing at once, standing alone and existing in its own time period. The foundation of this intricate web lies in a special gem that acts as the nucleus. Should the gem become damaged, irreparable damage can be done to the web. Causing it to weaken and tear, allowing for crossover between the —"

"Careful, now."

"But should the heart of the web, contained within a—"

"AH! Shush shuh-shhhhhhh! Shhhh!" the latter voice sputtered. "See? *That.* That right there is why you don't get to narrate."

"What are you going on about, now?"

"You can't just give away all the details at once. This is a journey. You want to unfold details as the story progresses. That way the audience has a chance to say, 'Oooh, aaaah.'"

"But then they won't have the basic foundation of which this Universe is based on!" The voice's already treacherous lilt now turned its owner's righteous indignation into petulant whining. "They'll get confused!"

"You can't give away the plot of the story during the introduction."

"True, but you still want the audience to understand how things flow and how they can potentially flow."

The void itself seemed to reverberate as a long-suffering sigh escaped the second, older-and-wiser voice. "Why don't I finish up from here? Here, use this to take notes. Watch how I am appropriately vague when I speak." It took a moment to dramatically clear its throat before beginning in an impressive, booming voice. "Even we gods do not understand everything. In this Universe lies a delicate and intricate web that holds many worlds together. These worlds contain beings that exists in different dimensions. For millennia, these worlds managed to secretly exist among each other, with only a select few knowing of their existence . . ."

"Such a control freak," the former groused under its divine breath. "Everything has to be done *your* way, doesn't it?"

"It is uncertain how this web functions —"

"Oh, COME ON." The first, younger voice couldn't contain itself any longer. "We absolutely know how this web functions!"

"Several theories speculated by the gods circulate throughout the Universe—"

"So, we're lying to them, to the audience? Is that how it works?"

"No." The single syllable sounded as if it might explode.

"Shouldn't we tell them this is a Universe with a multi-god system?"

"You know what? Here." Had there been a table in the void along with the two voices, the second one would have slammed its celestial hands onto it in defeat. "This is a story about a Universe that contains multiple worlds. The beings who live in this Universe have no idea these other worlds exist. There is a spider-like web that connects these worlds together. There may or may not be a rip in this web. There may or may not be crossover between these worlds. This may or may not be a comedic love story. Come for the plot, stay for the hot, sexy love story. This'll be hoot."

The first voice was silent with awe and admiration. "I think that was perfect."

"That was *far* from perfect. It took nearly four pages to give the introduction! It *should* have only taken a few paragraphs! I— Fine, fine. I'll take the compliment."

It fell silent and, for several minutes, neither seemed to know what to do.

"Um, I'm still a bit new at this. I don't really know how to, you know, make my exit. Do we just, what, poof?"

"Ah, yes. Just like this."

And, with that, the void returned to being the void.

Worlds Collide: Gods' Play

Written by

Estee Lee-Mountel & K.N. Nguyen

Original concept by

Millie Jean Warren

Tap, *tap.* Is this thing on? Ah, okay. Perhaps I should take things up from here since our, um, illustrious *gods* don't seem terribly interested in telling this story properly. It's probably because they don't really want to share their secrets, despite how much gods love talking about themselves and what they do. They're especially fond of showing off their godliness since they can do stuff we puny mortals obviously can't. It's a huge riot to them.

Now that those two are done bickering, we can really get to the meat of things.

They mentioned this gem, right? The foundation. The nexus, the crux, the end-all-be-all of this Universe, all official-looking with its capital U.

Well, the thing is, the gem was supposed to be the beginning *and* end; it was just supposed to... be. But where would our story be if that was the case? It all starts with a couple of younger gods who wanted to strut their stuff. Again, this is just what gods do, wanting to one-up each other. How do a couple of upstart gods try to show their divine prowess? By creating a fascinating, powerful gem!

I'm afraid it's all downhill from there.

Instead of listening to me prattle on about history, however, why don't we just rewind the universal clock a bit and see how everything went down for ourselves? Our story begins with the two would-be creators, wandering—and kvetching—through the great, vaunted halls of wherever it is that gods have yet another very important meeting (honestly, they're worse than politicians)...

Here, we meet our two younger deities, 15 and 16, because even all-powerful pantheons can be rather uncreative with their naming conventions. 15, the elder of the pair, is gesturing adamantly and very likely swearing.

*****

15: Sixteen! Can you believe what the Elders told us?

16: Believe it? Yes. Like it? No.

15: How can they be so presumptuous as to think that we cannot properly manage the Universe?! We're just as capable as those old crones are.

16: *[mimicking 4]* I'm *twelve* above you, *Sixteen!* I know best. Nyah nyah nyah! What does Four know, anyway? Being earlier in the line of existence doesn't make it any wiser or better at management. In fact, *I* think it makes one slower on the uptake. Instincts aren't as sharp as they used to be and all that, you know.

15: *[Putting on a haughty, pompous tone in imitation of 7]* Mmmm, yes. Four is quite right. After all, Four is one of the Originators.

16: Oh, DON'T EVEN GET ME STARTED. "Originators!" What kind of a stuck-up clique name is that? It's just about the most ridiculous thing I've ever heard.

15: Right? They think that since we weren't of the original five, we know nothing. We should show them how little they know.

16: The next five are just as bad, if not worse, because they actually buy into the whole "Originator" thing.

15: Especially Eight. Everything the Five say is Truth™ to Eight. It's so sickening how Eight questions NOTHING!

16: *[in a mocking falsetto, hands clasped dramatically next to face with eyes fluttering]* Oh, Five! What a GREAT idea! Oh, Five, tell me again how you came into existence and helped create the universe. Oh, Five!! *[ends in gagging noises]*

15: Oh Five! Let me polish thy feet!

16: *[muttering]* Probably polishes something else, if you know what I mean.

15: *[breaks into laughter]* Lights and Void, what a joke they all are.

16: *[sighs]* So, you dragged me out here for a reason, Fifteen. I assume it was for something other than saving me from their inane droning?

15: What would you say if we could show the Elders that we're more than just their underlings?

16: I'm listening.

15: I heard that Thirteen created a new star and it caught the attention of Two. What if we create more than a star? What if we create a *moon*?!

(16 raises a divine eyebrow and tilts its head— listening and considering.)

15: It could orbit *[REDACTED]*, their very seat of power, and those vain Elders can bask in the glory of our creation!

16: *[frowning now]* Yeah, but everyone knows thermonuclear fusion is much more complex than smashing together a bunch of rocks made from molecules. It'd be like watching Twenty make little "worms" from pliant dirt. *[more resolutely]* Besides, if they knew we did it, they'd all be shaking their heads, tut-tutting, and saying, "That's no moon..."

15: But if we can get Two or Three to appreciate it, we have a chance! Two and Three are the most reasonable of the Originators.

16: That's true...

15: It's worth a shot.

16: I don't know. I still feel like we need something more... *spectacular*.

15: Oh? Such as?

16: Well, for starters, a moon doesn't do much.

(15 slumps a bit and begins to look rather dejected.)

16: In fact, a moon would just be an ironic symbol of how we're always on the fringes, always cursed to orbit around the whims and desires of the "Originators." *[sees the now defeated-looking 15]* Oh come now, don't look so glum! First ideas are always just the beginning!

15: But what can we create to show them we're just as capable? A star will eventually die.

16: Ooh ooh, I know! What if that moon could create... Uh... *[thinks hard, scrambling for ideas]*... OTHER MOONS?!

15: *[gasps]*

16: We can teach the elements and molecules to self-replicate into other matter! I'd bet even One hasn't accomplished that! *[looks rather proud of self]*

15: Do you think we can do that?

16: *[pauses in preening, thinking]* Sure we can. We're gods after all, aren't we? *[snaps fingers and creates a delicious pastry]*

15: *[imitating 8 again]* Mmmm yes, we are. And damn good ones at that. *[shakes head politely at proffered pastry]* Ah, no thanks. You know I'm watching my figure.

16: *[shrugs]* More for me!

15: *[imitating 4]* You younger generations don't understand the difficulties of us Elders. We can't maintain our commanding figures by magic. *[chuckles]* If we're not careful, we'll end up like Six.

16: They did make Six their chef. It kind was kind of inevitable.

15: But *they* can't be blamed for anything.

16: Of course not. It'd shake the entire foundation of our order.

15: It's almost as though they're gods or something *[laughs]*

16: *[laughs in kind]*

15: *[runs hand through hair]* So, we're going to create a self-sustaining, self-preserving entity?

16: And self-replicating! It might get lonely, after all.

15: Right, right.

16: We better get a move on. Those old crones have a way of staying in that chamber and prattling on at one another.

15: Not if Nine is with them. *[winks]*

16: Aww, come now. I kinda like Nine. It's not *all* that bad.

15: I agree. Nine and Ten are actually the best of the second generation. But all joking aside, now, I think we have a solid plan here.

16: You know of the best places to go. Where do you think we should go so we can do our work undisturbed?

15: Hmmm, how about the temporal plane? If I were to create— for lack of better word— life, I would want there to be warmth to help with the growth.

16: Tricky, but I think it would actually make our experimentation easier. Fewer constraints and a little more concreteness.

15: Exactly.

16: This is why we're best friends, Fifteen; great intelligences think alike! Let's go! *[poofs away as 15 does likewise]*

(*In the temporal plane, our two deities are quickly gathering up atoms and molecules. The phrase "mad scientist" comes to mind as we rejoin these eager immortals.*)

15: What do you think of adding some oxygen? I think it's pretty helpful for replication.

16: That's a good one. Maybe some nitrogen to balance it out.

15: A bit of Carbon. *[pauses, eyeballing the concoction]* Ehh... Let's add more. Never enough carbon.

16: Carbon-based life form seems like the easier, better route, if you ask me. Remember 13's experiment with silicone? *[shudders]*

15: Oh yeah. Let's avoid that disaster. *[continues putting things together]* Hydrogen? Oh! Maybe some iron!

16: Of course! Can't get by without the basics.

15: Calcium, too, to help strengthen the shell.

16: We *are* going to have to add just a little of silicon.

15: Just a hint. *[suddenly looks at something behind 16]* Hey!

16: *[looking around, confused]* What?

15: What's in that bottle? *[points at green bottle over 16's shoulder]* Was there always a bottle here?

16: Which one? This one? I thought you brought that along for a drink.

15: Oh no. I'm abstaining during our week of Lifting.

16: *[uncertainly to self]* I don't know about this...

15: *[pops cork out of bottle]* Well, whatever it is, it can't hurt to add a smidge.

16: ... You know I don't partake at all. So, if it's not yours and it's not mi— HEY! Are you sure that's a good idea?

15: I don't think anything could go—

(A very large and very loud and very startling explosion occurs. Our two deities look rather out of sorts but they're none the worse for wear because, after all, they're immortals.)

16: *[groans]* What. Was. THAT?!

15: Ugh. *[rubs head tenderly]* My eye, my eye! There's something in my eye! *[taps injured eye with a finger]* Ah, much better. Maybe that was a bad idea...

16: I don't think we can regret anything now. Look! *[ogles]*

15: *[turns around uncertainly]* Huh?

16: It's certainly... *shiny*.

*(Both turn around to see that, where they once set up their experiment, now stood a perfectly crafted **gem**. It's suspended in the temporal plane like it's powered by a dynamo. Ethereal light plays along **the gem's** multiple facets. They've never seen anything quite like it before in any of the planes.)*

15: *[blinks disbelievingly]* Blinding Lights! Did we actually create something?

16: I think we did! *[ecstatically hugs 15]*

15: *[whoops with glee and returns the congratulatory hug from 16]* I can't believe we actually did it!

16: It's... It's gorgeous! Just look at it! It's even finer than some of One's more ostentatious costumes!

15: It is! Wait. Look closer. Do you see something... *moving?*

16: Is that... Wait, is it actually creating... *something else?*

15: Hey, there's another one over there! And there!

16: And a big one over there! *[coughs]* Not that, uh, size matters or anything.

15: And *FAUNA?*

16: *[looking clearly pleased and happy]* And biomes! Wait, this thing we've created is actually making its own *worlds!* Fully sustained and complete worlds!

15: Lights and Void, I think we created LIFE!

16: In multitudes!

15: *[groaning in growing displeasure]* What did we do? This is *not* good.

16: Wait, what? Isn't this a good thing? This is what we were going for wasn't it? Oh man, this is gonna knock the socks right off of—

15: No.

16: *[a bit crestfallen]* Oh.

15: You know the Elders. They don't like to do anything other than be worshipped. They'll make us care for this, this universe.

16: *[optimistically]* Maybe we can teach the beings down there to worship them.

15: *[thoughtfully]* That would be a good idea.

16: It's not just one planet, but a WHOLE universe of new worshippers!

15: *[slowly warming to the idea]* That's an even better idea...

16: It would make One and Four's heads explode from their overgrown egos!

15: *[staring at the glowing **gem** dreamily]* I *would* love to see Four's head explode...

16: And One might even overlook that we made something shinier than it.

15: *[snapping out of reverie]* Maybe. *[suddenly self-conscious]* Do you think they'll be impressed? I mean, Two *has* to be impressed with life. It is LIFE, after all.

16: Oh, come on— a self-replicating, self-sustaining, self-EVERYTHING entity! It's going to absolutely knock their divine socks off.

15: Right, right. *[brightens]* Come on, let's show them.

*(The two reappear in the halls where their elders are likely still droning on and on about something, gingerly carrying their **gem** and its precious creations.)*

16: Should we just walk in?

15: *[stops, suddenly nervous]* I... I think so.

16: They probably didn't even notice we were gone.

15: No, that would require them to pay attention to what's going on around them.

16: *[muttering]* And look beyond their massive egos.

15: That'll be the day. Or should I say, *today* will be the day. *[resolutely]* Let's go.

16: *[holds open the massive door]* After you, Fifteen!

*(The two enter a room inhabited by the **Five Originators**, 7, 8, and 10.)*

4: What are you two doing in this room? Don't you know that this is *our* personal room?

(16 nudges 15 encouragingly.)

15: Well, we would like to show you something that we think will make your lives even more interesting.

16: *[brightly]* We made it ourselves.

*(15 motions for 16 to reveal **the gem**. 16 holds up **the gem** to the light for all to behold. There's a slight murmur of interest from the gods. 2 and 3 seem to be the only ones who are genuinely interested and not afraid to show it, however.)*

16: *[looking around, rather awkwardly]* Well?

15: Here, allow me to show off some of its incredible features. It's self-replicating, self-sustaining—

2: What possessed you two to create something like this? *[gets up and hovers around 15 and 16, examining **the gem**]*

16: Well, I... uh... we... *[suddenly annoyed at the others' ambivalence]* Aren't you even the slightest bit impressed?! It's got its own WORLDS, for crying out loud! Unique life forms and fauna and biomes and...!

4: Of course not! Why would we be impressed by a mere gem?

2: Oh Lights and Void, Four. This is incredible!

15: They also seem to have inhabitants— inhabitants who could be persuaded to worship a greater deity, or *deities*...

4: *[who was still rambling while 15 spoke]* And what would *we* possibly have to— Oh? You don't say...

3: I must say, this is quite impressive.

15: *[hurriedly]* Yes!

16: Just imagine it, you guys...

15: As an... honor for our Elders, we wanted to present something worthy of your greatness.

16: Not just one world but a MULTITUDE of them. Just waiting for the right pantheon of gods *[gestures to the Originators]* to come and show their feeble mortal minds just how incredible they are.

(The sound of a throat being cleared can be heard, faintly yet distinctly. 1 remains seated as it speaks. All eyes turn to 1, and everyone quiets out of respect.]

1: I understand that you wanted to try your hands at something grand. *[raises eyebrow slightly]*

16: *[defiantly]* I don't think we just *tried*. We *succeeded*.

1: However, you seem to have miscalculated this: while it is nice to have supplicants, we are quite busy and do not need more responsibility at this time.

15: But, One—

1: *[holds up hand to silence 15]* The effort is appreciated, but not something that is worthy of interrupting our quiet time.

(1 dismisses 15 and 16 with a stately, single gesture.)

15: *[crestfallen]* But...

16: Fine.

*(Indignant, 16 snatches **the gem** back and turns on its heel to leave. 15 slowly retreats and follows after. Once out of the chamber, 15 begins to fume. 16 is muttering darkly under its divine breath.)*

15: Lights and Void! We almost had them. Two and Three were totally into it!

16: Forget them! If they can't appreciate this... this... this wonder of divine engineering, I'll... I'll... *[trails off, dejected]*

15: C'mon! Let's go back to our own plane. *[grabs **the gem** and throws it down on the ground]* Leave this. I don't want to see it anymore.

16: *[waving frantically]* Whoa whoa WHOA! Don't—

*(**The gem** skitters down the hall. A small explosion sounds from the direction of **the gem**. 15 and 16 glance uncertainly at one another, then look down the hall.)*

16: Oh great. Now you've done it. I mean, I know you're mad and all but there was life on those worlds! Who knows what could have happened to them by throwing the gem around like that! *[runs to retrieve and examine **the gem**]*

15: I'm sorry. It's just so frustrating! *[peering at **the gem** very closely]* Is everything okay?

16: I think so. The gem looks like it's cracked, though. There are all these weird, glowy, spindly lines.

15: Oh Lights, I'm sorry. *[walks closer]* Huh? They're radiating out from the gem.

16: Hold on a second. They're *in* the gem.

15: *In* it?!

16: And they seem to be connecting the worlds. *[eyes widening in slow understanding]* Oh. My. Lights. And. Void. Wow.

15: What?! Are they... uniting the worlds?

16: Yup. The worlds: they're all connected. And the gem's the only thing sustaining all of this. If something were to happen to the gem... *[trails off ominously]*

15: *[speechlessly staring at 16 in awe]*

16: Who knows what would happen to the inhabitants of those worlds?

15: *[whispers]* What did we do?

16: *[barely audible]* I don't even know. This is... This is way beyond my paygrade. *[shoves **gem** to 15]*

15 *[shoving **the gem** back]* Psh, I don't want it!

16: Hey, hey!! GENTLY. Geez. *[cradles **the gem**]* Who knows what would happen if we disturb it further?! Let's just... Let's find a safe place for this and, uh, not tell the others. Sound good?

15: *[looks around furtively]* Agreed.

*****

And that's how this all got started. Now, don't you feel better about your own seemingly accidental existence?

About the Authors

Nicholas Walls

Nicholas Walls is an author, educator, and storyteller. Inspired by tales of dragons and knights, and usually siding with the dragons, Nicholas has been telling tales and writing for many years. Over the course of earning his Masters of Art in History, he's had many chances to practice his craft. Yet a good tale untold, is as of little use of as knowledge unshared. So Nicholas began working with DragonScript to spread awesome stories and inspire others to follow their dreams.

Nicholas Walls is also the founder and produce of History-In-5, a muli-platform social media website designed to share knowledge about and inspire interest in History, with engaging tales.

He also offers research, writing, and editorial skills via Fiverr account at www.fiverr.com/nicholaswalls.

K.N. Nguyen

K.N. Nguyen began her early years participating in sports year round, studying biology and creating imaginary worlds to play in. After reading *The Chronicles of Narnia*, her mind was opened and new worlds were created. These stories tantalized her imagination and kindled a desire to begin writing. As the years passed, she started studying ancient mythology and reading more epic fantasies. After several failed attempts at writing a fantasy novel, she gave it up as a lost cause. It wasn't until she started working at her office job that she felt the itch to begin writing again. Once taking up the pen, things seemed to click and the first of her *Fallen* trilogy was born. From this trilogy, she co-founded DragonScript, her own self-publishing company, to help her realize her dream of building worlds. It is her hope to be able to inspire others to follow their dreams as did the authors who inspired her.

T. M. Lowe

 T. M. Lowe was an aspiring writer from Jacksonville, Florida, when her mother took her own life in 2012. Mrs. Lowe stopped following her lifelong passion while trying to figure out how to cope with the sudden, unexpected loss. Four years later, she determined to take up writing again in her mother's memory. Her short stories contained within are her first published works.

Mrs. Lowe is 31 years old and currently resides in St. Augustine, Florida, with her husband and household of rescued animals. When not writing, her hobbies include playing video games, watching her beloved Florida Gators play football in the fall, reading, watching dirt track racing, fishing, and shooting pool while drinking whiskey in smoky dive bars.

To catch updates on her current writing projects, follow her on Twitter at @TiffanyMLowe or visit her Facebook page at www.facebook.com/AuthorTMLowe.

Estee Lee-Mountel

Estee, a native Californian, started off in professional writing as a journalist, including narrative non-fiction pieces for *Sacramento News & Review*. Her goals are rooted in telling the stories of and educating people. She currently guides people to knowledge as a library services assistant in Cincinnati, OH, using what little free time she has for writing, video/tabletop gaming, cosplay, and various other crafts. This is her first foray into writing and publishing fiction.

And, in case you're wondering how Estee ended up in the Midwest: she met her husband, a native of Cincinnati, in *World of Warcraft*. They have two kids.

You can follow her oft-punny and nerdy musings on Twitter at @Toriah_the_Mom.

Photo/art credit: Caricature self-portrait by the author.

Millie Jean Warren

Millie Jean Warren makes her living working as a performer in the San Francisco and Sacramento areas. She also owns and operates Parties Galore (www.partiesgaloreca.com), a company that provides costumed characters to entertain children at birthday parties. While her interest and focus is predominately in front of the camera, her love for live audience interaction keeps her rooted in the theatre. Millie's fascination with screenplays, characters and visual entertainment fueled her interest in branching out into the world of cartoons. As she works on her first screenplay "Worlds Collide," Millie plans to venture into the zany world of cartoon heroes. Her goal, as an actor and writer, is to inspire the world and its people to connect and laugh with one another.

Acknowledgements from T. M. Lowe

To my husband, Jason Lowe, for always believing in me and for holding me up when I felt too weak to go on; for giving me advice I needed to hear and for always being by my side; for pulling me up when I'm down in a hole and for showing me how to punch the world back harder when it's punched me in the mouth; and for putting up with many nights and weekends of being a writer's widower while I stare at my laptop screen.

To my father, Rick Myers, for influencing so much of my life; for being the basis of my clone-dom; and for always supporting me and knowing I would make a mark on the world.

To my late mother, Holly Myers, who was my first cheerleader and my biggest supporter. Her death threw me severely off-pace, but I keep trudging through in her memory.

To my late grandparents, Anne and Thomas Darby, who encouraged my creativity from a very young age.

To the BioWare team that created and maintained Mass Effect 3 Multiplayer. Every last one of you, whether you are still with the company or elsewhere. It was your creation that breathed the first bit of fun back into my life in the wake of my mother's suicide and it was that small beacon of hope that allowed me to crawl through the desert of my grief and back into some semblance of normalcy and creativity. Forever and always, the deepest of my gratitude for making me smile and laugh again.

To Estee, my friend who alerted me to this short story anthology not long after I'd made it known that my 2016 New Year's Resolution was to force myself back into writing again to try and regain that spark of creativity, to either find my old muse or gain a new one.

To K.N. Nguyen, for organizing this entire venture and being gracious enough to allow me to participate when she did not know me from Adam.

To my friends, "Red" and Dr. John Worz, who both provided direct inspiration for "The Lady and the Dragon."

To everyone else who has touched my life, be it family or friends; I love you all dearly and each of you has had an impact on me and my writing.

Acknowledgements from K.N. Nguyen

To my parents, Kaylyn and Earl Warren, I would like to thank you for always encouraging me to reach for whatever goal I set within my sights. Even when I fell short, you always motivated me to pick myself up and move forward instead of give up.

To my loving husband, Francis, I would like to thank you for all that you've done while I organized this venture. Not only did you continually support me as I balanced both my career and my writing, but you also volunteered to format the anthology and prepare it for publication. Without all of your hard work, this anthology would not be what it is today.

To my fellow authors who helped me realize a life-long dream, I would like to thank T. M. Lowe, Estee, Nick and Millie Jean. Each of you have played an integral part in building this anthology and I am forever grateful for all of your efforts.

To all of my friends, I would like to thank you for all of your support and positive words. You've helped push me forward in this endeavor.

Both Estee Lee-Mountel and I would also like to thank Mr. York, our high school AP English teacher, who didn't flunk us outright for 'Cyclops: The Musical,' which only encouraged us to create more abominations as seen in this anthology.

Acknowledgements from Estee Lee-Mountel

To my mom and late father, who gave me the structure, discipline, and space to grow into the person I wanted to be, and always took the time to look at my doodles and scribbles.

To my husband, Chuck, who is my rock and cheerleader. Thanks for keeping me grounded while I panicked and groused and, sometimes, finally found the right words.

To my kids, the Whelpling and the Broodling, who inspire me to be someone they could brag about to their friends. You know, aside from, "*My* mom can find the answer to anything in ten seconds flat with multiple sources and citations!"

To my parents-in-law, Margaret and Dick, who always listen to my latest endeavors and never fail to support me with genuine excitement and encouragement.

To my brother, Eeden, who had to put up with me as we grew up. (Well, I grew up, anyway. The jury's still out about him, though.) Thanks for introducing me to the worlds of Tolkien, Douglas Adams, and *Wing Commander*.

To K.N. Nguyen, who's been my creative partner-in-crime since freshman year of high school. To think that all of this started with Shakespeare's

Romeo and Juliet in Mrs. Callahan's Advanced English 9 and, "HARK! Thy naked weapon is out!"

To T. M. Lowe, who is easily one of the kindest and most talented people I have the privilege of knowing. She's proof that video games— with a solid community like the one we're a part of— *are* good for something.

To Blizzard and BioWare, who taught me that good storytelling with immersive narratives are never out of fashion.

To Ms. Lynette Chertorisky, my fifth grade teacher, who saw the potential in me and never let me forget about that potential, either. When she heard I couldn't make it to the Young Authors' Awards because I didn't have a ride, she personally drove both my mother and me to the celebration. She taught me so much more than simple academics.

To Mrs. Susan Higgins, my eighth grade English teacher, who refused to let the death of my father put out my creative spark or hold me back. I never would have made it onto the bus for that pivotal Shakespeare trip in Ashland, Oregon if not for her assistance.

To Mrs. Pamela McPike, my tenth grade English teacher and faculty advisor for the campus newspaper, who was my very first editor and adamantly swore that *Les Miserables* should never EVER be shortened to *Les Mis.*

To the educators, staff, and faculty, all too numerous to name individually, who have influenced me from grade school to university; to countless friends and members of my community; to my work family at the library— Thank you. You have no idea just how much you factor into all of this.

www.ingramcontent.com/pod-product-compliance
Lightning Source LLC
Chambersburg PA
CBHW060545310726
48982CB00009B/1379/J